King of the Hoboes

King of the Hoboes

John Reinhard Dizon

Published 2016 by Creativia

Book design by Creativia (www.creativia.org)

Cover Design by http://www.thecovercollection.com/

Chapter One

Veronika Heydrich was a liar.

It was her fatal flaw, the demon that followed her all the days of her life. They called it storytelling when she was a little girl, fibbing in grade school, and exaggerating in high school. During her University days they called it her Heydrich spin, and as an undercover cop they called it a natural gift. Only it had made a wreck of her personal life and destroyed almost every relationship she ever had. She was the kind of girl who could swear on all she held dear and look you straight in the eye while lying through her teeth. She crushed many people throughout her life who thought they had come with her to the moment of truth, only to have her renege in an ultimate betrayal. For them it was a bridge burned forever, for her it was just another sad episode in the story of her life.

She had been a mistress at rationalization, perhaps her greatest sin, her ability to lie to herself. She made herself believe that she was better off having severed relationships with those who could not help her get ahead, those who expected to suffer a setback in favor of truth. She could not think of a single situation where the lie could not have eventually become the truth, where she had not been able to prevail by turning fantasy into reality. She could not think of one person who had walked away from her who had truly become a loss in her life.

Actually there was one. Evan Carlow had walked away, and her partner turned lover turned fiancée turned rival had been missed. She had never gotten that close to a man before, and it was almost as if she had finally found her soulmate. They had moved in together, they had set a wedding date, but she just couldn't stop lying and he finally had enough. When he moved out he took a piece of her heart with him, and she realized she had to get him back so she could put herself back together.

They had been partners on the field, and they voluntarily split up to assist on separate sting operations for the NYPD. Police Chief Joel Madden had been her guardian angel throughout her career, and he knew that giving her and Carlow some space was the best thing for them. Everyone knew they had a personal relationship, and they were true professionals who left it at home when they put on their badges in the morning. He also knew they were one of his best undercover teams, and he hoped it was going to work out to the benefit of the NYPD. Veronika knew it would be to her benefit as well.

There had been rumors about a police investigation developing over the homeless movement in New York City as an estimated sixty thousand persons listed were being recruited into an activist movement. IMU, or I Am You, had become a rallying cry that began on Facebook, then began appearing on patches and stickers appearing on backpacks and shopping carts among the destitute. At first it was seen as a reproach to the affluent, but recently there were concerns that a militant group had professed an ulterior motive.

Word had spread that the King of the Hoboes, Adolf Hyatt, had come to NYC with the express purpose of uniting the homeless of New York in an activist movement. Hyatt had been allegedly crowned as King of the hobo underground network that had existed for over two hundred years. Members of the network had been interviewed over the decades, and it was seen as an exotic facet of Americana unique to its society and culture. Artists and poets across the decades had extolled the traveling spirit of wanderers across the country, and 'riding the rails' was stuff that legends were made of. Only the thought of homeless people uniting in a militant cause was alarming people still experiencing the long-term effects of 9/11.

Police activity among the homeless was not unusual. It was a running joke among the law enforcement community that every other vagrant on the streets of Washington DC was most likely a Secret Service agent.

However, the eyes of the law had not been trained on the homeless themselves as persons of interest. It was an exceedingly unpleasant task in the eyes of NYPD officials, who foresaw a multitude of problems should the investigation come to light.

The prevailing concern was that humanitarian groups might withdraw their support for the homeless community, which would cause greater stress on an already overburdened social services system. There was also the crisis issue regarding the skyrocketing number of families and at-risk children who were on the streets with no permanent place of residence. The NYPD would be loathe to demonize them as a side effect of a campaign against a rogue group whose existence had not officially been confirmed.

Veronika had been flipping through the case files as she made coffee and toast in her kitchenette in her SoHo loft on Prince Street. She loved the neighborhood and the local ambiance, a world apart from her upper-class beginnings in Southampton. From the time she enrolled at New York University and pursued her degree in law enforcement, she knew that this was the place where she belonged. It greatly helped her develop her chameleon skills, as she convinced most people she was an aspiring starlet complete with a resume she had developed by way of a string of auditions she had with different off-Broadway theatre groups. No one ever suspected her of being a cop, and those who crossed from one of her worlds to another were generally sworn to secrecy.

The phone rang, and her heart leaped when she saw it was Evan on caller ID. She raced across the living room and rolled across her convertible sofa, snatching it from the charger before he hung up on the recorded message.

"Evan."

"Hey, beautiful, how's it going?"

"I don't like that you hang up without leaving a message. I practically have to tackle the phone just to talk to you. I do have a cell phone, you know."

"I don't do messages or cell phones unless it's an emergency, you know that. Anyway, did you decide if we were gonna bid on the job?"

"I don't know, Evan. It's a filthy environment and disgusting people. It was bad enough having to mingle with those geeks during that hacker case, let alone those gangbangers in that crack gang. Now you're wanting to disguise us as a couple of bums."

"Well, check this out. I talked to Lieutenant Shreve this morning. He had a long discussion with Captain Willard the other day. They're pretty sure that if this job goes over, you'll get upped. Chief Madden will probably put you in for a gold badge."

"Oh my gosh, Evan, that's fantastic!" she gushed. "Well, I guess there's nothing left to discuss. Let's do it."

"There's a lot to talk about before we commit to this," he insisted. "There's a lot we don't know—*nobody* knows—about these people. It's a complex, multicultural society with lots of distinctive protocols and behavioral patterns. Murder is just as much a way of life with some of these people as it is for the Mafia or any other gang culture. Most of these people live day to day, hand to mouth, and betrayal can be considered a capital offense. If they find out we're conning them, our lives could easily be at risk."

"We spent months taking down a crack gang whose signature mark was leaving informers with their throats slit in the middle of the street," Veronika went back into the kitchen and poured herself a cup of coffee before buttering her toast. "I should think that we will be at far less risk amidst a bunch of bums."

"Problem is, you wouldn't know who's bringing it, who it's from or where they're going," Evan insisted. "At least when you think a gangster's looking for you, you can see it coming. You can defend yourself. Do you think we can get set every time somebody dressed like shit turns the corner? Even worse, if they do make the hit, they might never be brought to justice. How do you find someone who has no identification, no address, no background? It's a serious problem, and they want you to know there will be serious risks."

"I'm in, Evan. They put that gold badge on the table and I'm in. Look, I'll meet you at your place at noon."

She ate her breakfast, then stripped for her shower as she checked herself in the mirror. She was a big girl, standing 5'8" and 140 pounds, a classic Nordic beauty with thick blonde waist-long hair. She had a knockout figure with a large bosom, a 24-inch waist and well-muscled things and calves. She had narrow, ice-blue eyes that seemed cruel at times, offset by thick lips that were quick to smile at her advantage. She made it a point to go to the gym twice a week and ate what she called rabbit food when by herself to keep her hourglass figure. She knew her beauty had a lot to do with her getting ahead in life, and did whatever it took to keep her running in the fast lane.

She threw on a black jumpsuit, white sneakers and shades, tied her hair back in a loose bun, and headed down to the street for a quick run up to Washington Square Park and back so as to be on time to meet Evan at his Gramercy Park apartment. Veronika saw it as another subtle difference between them, the plainclothes cop and the undercover detective. She was making it in SoHo at fifty grand, while Evan was living in one of the more prestigious neighborhoods in town with his $90k salary. She was the one taking the risks, playing the point and sticking her neck out, while he was the lifeline always ready to pull her out of a jam. She decided it was time for her to get paid for the risks she was taking, time to collect the gold star.

As she jogged along, she never failed to notice how there was not a whole lot of peace and joy in the faces of the people on the street. She always knew it was a struggle to make it in New York, as far back as her first days at NYU. She remembered how most of her schoolmates did their best to make ends meet with part-time jobs and care packages from home. When she joined the NYPD and left home shortly before her father died, her inheritance and new salary were enough to get her into a SoHo loft. Still, it was no cakewalk. When the home in Southampton was sold, there was no nest to fly home to. Yet, she was not going to become one of the cheerless masses. She found her place and she would keep it at all costs.

Meeting Evan was one of the highpoints of her post-graduate life. He was a full-blooded Irishman just as she was one hundred percent German. He brought much of his ethnic charm and high-spiritedness into their relationship, just as she maintained her German sense of order and stoic determination. They became a formidable team on the field when Captain Ty Willard first teamed them up. When the partnership blossomed into romance, they tried to keep it quiet at work as best they could. Only Evan eventually had to declare his position to protect it against the alpha males that abounded throughout the force. They spent most of their time together on the field and off, but at the break of dawn they each went back to their own home.

She understood the need for freedom, what the old-school Germans called *lebensraum*. She put a lock on her door back home as a teenager, and lived a model life in an immaculate room as compensation to her parents. Yet she would have given it all away if her privacy had been taken from her, and her parents knew and respected that. Evan knew it as well, and if he had given her an ultimatum to move in with him, he would have lost her forever. He knew that she would come into his home at the time of her choosing, and he knew the wait would be well worth it.

The bums on the street knew the price of freedom. So did the teenage mothers wheeling their kids along in their cheap, ragged strollers. They could have headed South and found a city where the cost of living was much lower, and the assisted living was much more dignified. Yet when they woke up, they would not see the NYC skyline, experience the Big Apple hustle and bustle. This was the greatest city on earth, and a bum would die broke and starved beneath a bridge than leave it behind. It kept students in cold-water flats living on Ramen, and unwed mothers collecting welfare with a State-issued piece of plastic as the only thing in their purse. New York got to be part of one's DNA, and Veronica knew what that was all about.

She reached Evan's apartment and used her key to get in, hearing him playing Irish folk music on his sound system from outside. She tried playing German folk music a few times to get some equal time on principle, but it didn't work for either of them so she gave up. She really didn't care what background noise was going on. She was mostly about the constant search for information, building databases on whatever case they were working on at the time. She liked being able to throw facts and figures around at Department meetings, forever reminding them that they were far from dealing with just another pretty face.

"Well, look who's back," he yawned and stretched as he reclined on the living room sofa. Evan was a handsome man with dark hair, blue eyes and a muscular build. He was slightly taller than Veronika at 5'10", and most agreed they made a perfect couple. He was also wearing a jogging suit, as they were of like mind that it kept one dressed for any occasion.

"I'm going to take a shower," she announced, pulling off her sweatshirt to expose her luscious melons straining against her sports bra. "I suppose we'd better start putting our proposal on paper to submit to Captain Willard sometime today."

"Good morning honey, how are you this morning?" Evan replied sarcastically. "Have you had breakfast yet?"

"Just ran it off," she was in the bathroom turning on the shower.

"Time for a bit of the old in-out, in-out?" he sauntered over to the doorway.

"Go screw yourself for a change," she replied. "Close the door, you're letting the steam out. I hope there's one clean towel in here."

"Well, I'm making bacon and eggs with tarragon."

"Drive down to Mc Donald's, leave it to the experts."

"Good, you're not getting any," he pulled the door closed.

"Yeah, we'll see."

She eventually emerged from the shower with a towel wrapped around her hair, wearing her terrycloth robe. She walked into the kitchen and found a cup of hot coffee, a plate of eggs and bacon with tarragon on a tortilla, and a small glass of milk on the table. Next to it was a five-page report.

"How nice," she muttered as he sat in the living room, channel-surfing his plasma TV. She sighed with contentment as she took a bite of her taco, savoring its flavor before gobbling everything down so she could read the report.

"I can bring it in and drop it off when we take off," Even called in over the commentary of a pre-taped hockey game.

"You got typos," she pored over it. "All this without my help. Fascinating."

"Don't get smart, missy. Good to go?" he called back.

"Well, if it was a choice between the taco and the report, I'd go with the taco," she came into the living room, licking her fingers. "I don't this Willard will appreciate the taco as much, so we'd best turn in the report."

"Smart ass, eh?" he rolled off the couch and cornered her by the bookcase. "Come here."

"Stay back," she warned him. "I just took a shower."

"I've slept on the couch all night abusing myself over you. Now you're gonna pay for it."

"Hah! You think so?"

At once he took her into his arms and spun her down upon the shag carpet. She always liked to have control of just one thing, and grabbed his chin and his lips in both hands as he pulled his pants down. She opened his mouth and snaked her tongue inside, his lips to do with as she wished as he thrust himself deep inside her. She gasped with pain and pleasure as he began pumping her frantically, his passion increasing as she hungrily pillaged his mouth, trying to gently suck his tongue out of his skull.

The report that would change their lives forever sat in a small grease spot on the kitchen table behind them.

Chapter Two

Adolf Hyatt was known as the King throughout the Hobo Underground.

It was an unusual honor bestowed upon an unusual man. Traditionally, there was an annual hobo convention in Britt, Iowa, where hoboes from around the country converged to name a King and Queen at a weekend celebration of life on the rails. In real life, the leaders of the hobo network met at a designated place once a year to exchange information, appoint elder statesmen who could settle disputes and make policy, and crown a King. The King of the Hoboes was the ultimate authority when the regional leaders could not agree on a decision. Adolf Hyatt had never been called upon to settle a dispute, but wherever he went his word was law.

Hyatt was born in Alamogordo, New Mexico, and legend had it that his family's exposure to radiation during nuclear testing in the Fifties had endowed him with mutant powers. He bragged of a 160 IQ, had a photographic memory and retard strength. He also had the gift of preaching which he used to great advantage after leaving home at the age of eighteen to see America. It was said he could tell a story about a cat that would make a dog cry, and that he could sell ice to an Eskimo.

He also said that whoever controlled the streets controlled the city, and one day he would travel to New York City and show the homeless how it was done. On the day he arrived, a construction site in the South Bronx had become so congested by vagrants that the entire community stood in wonder. The mood of the vagabonds ranged from defensive to hostile, and even gang leaders throughout the area conveniently chose to ignore the event. By the time the police came out to inquire, the meeting dispersed so that there was not a bum in sight.

He next appeared at a warehouse near the Brooklyn Bridge that the Watchtower Society had donated to the homeless near Brooklyn Heights as a tax write-off. Hyatt turned it into his stronghold, and was soon confronted by Jehovah's Witnesses who demanded to know why one man and his twelve companions were the sole occupants of a shelter designed for two hundred. Hyatt assured them that he was spreading the word to the community, and that Saturday there were a dozen vagrants at every Kingdom Hall in Brooklyn. Not one Witness called upon Adolf Hyatt at the shelter thereafter.

The next thing advocates for the homeless knew, their target group was proclaiming a Day of Defiance on their new website, I-AM-YOU.com. It proclaimed that the homeless were a mirror image of mainstream society without the perks, the common man trying to make it in a world without advantages. The Site Administrator proclaimed that every homeless man was fighting for the rights of his brothers and sisters, just as Americans had fought for their freedom since the birth of the nation. He emphasized that not only did the homeless had an obligation to act, but the man of means had the same obligation to stand by the less fortunate.

Hyatt next sent out his twelve Disciples to recruit Followers who would help them spread the word throughout the homeless community. The Followers were to report back to their Disciple, and their mission was to find three Recruits of like mind. They would form a Cell from which they would eventually break off and form Cells of their own. At first everyone thought it would never work, but eventually realized they were already part of four-man groups that lived together under bridges, in back alleys and vacant lots on a daily basis. The Recruit stopped by and visited the Cell each day, and soon everyone was connected to Hyatt and knew what he was up to.

The Day of Defiance was all about the homeless community's chance to piss on society the same way society was pissing on them. It was also about the torment imposed upon the needy by depriving them of the most fundamental right that even an infant enjoyed. Outside of public parks and libraries, there was no place for a homeless person to take a piss, and heaven forbid they should have to take a shit. No Public Restrooms signs were taped on the doors and windows of every business, and taking a leak in the street cost thirty days in jail if caught by a cop. Pissing in one's pants was a temporary solution; cleaning one's pants was harder than taking the leak. The worst case scenario was getting seen pissing, which could result in a public exposure bust and a lifetime rap as a sex offender.

Each homeless person was asked to donate one baggie to the Day of Defiance. The baggie was to be filled with urine and deposited it in a place where it would do most good as a symbol of protest. It was suggested that the baggie be dumped onto a paper-filled target so that the odor could allow those of means to experience what many homeless people had to breathe in all night where they slept. If a paper target was not available, then doorways were suggested as the only place where most homeless people found shelter along with the familiar odor.

The Day started before dawn as vagrants waited until newspaper delivery trucks loaded their kiosks with the morning paper. The activists invested change to open the hatches and toss in their bags of urine. About an hour after sunrise, people on their way to work crowded around newsstands and stores to buy the morning paper as almost every kiosk on every block was drenched with urine. Many of them were alarmed by the fact that the storefronts smelled as well, making many think that perhaps they got some on their clothes when they made contact with the contaminated kiosks.

As the morning progressed, the media began reporting the trend of people calling in to report the stench of urine across many residential and commercial areas across Manhattan. Once homeless advocates began logging onto I-AM-U.com, they realized what was happening. They called the media's attention to Hyatt's vituperative attacks on the bourgeoisie and how they were creating a caste system as deplorable and inalterable as that in India. *Good Morning America* jumped all over the story, posing the question as to whether the website was helping or harming the homeless community with their militant stance. They also demanded to know the identity of the Site Administrator, wondering who he was and what his objective was in making such polarizing statements.

The worst impact was experienced in the subway system, where over a million commuters were forced to endure the stench caused by the baggie bombs. Ever since the days of Rudy Giuliani, the NYPD had strictly enforced a code of cleanliness in the subways. Those who pissed, spat, littered and caused noise pollution in the subways faced fines and even arrest. The police found themselves overwhelmed and caught unaware by the baggie bombardment, and were ordered to beef up their presence in public places to deter any further attacks.

As Hyatt had anticipated, those who bore the brunt of the public backlash were the homeless. The NYPD sent officers to soup kitchens and shelters around town, sermonizing those in attendance against participating in such actions and warning them of the consequences if they were caught. The homeless families and Iraqi veterans were particularly insulted by the insinuations, and even more so in learning that some facilities would be closed the next day to avoid any association with activists or social agitators.

Hyatt sent forth his cells to ensure homeless people around the City that they would stand in solidarity alongside their oppressed brethren, and that the Administration would pay dearly for any reprisals against vagrants for the iniquities of the few. His website declared that the homeless community would not tolerate any acts of aggression against their population, and retaliation against one would be considered an attack on all. He also intimated that the Day of Defiance might very well be replayed in the near future if vagrants were threatened anywhere.

The website further demanded that the City set up portable toilets at strategic areas around town so that such a thing need never happen again. The statement went viral as advocates for the underprivileged weighed in, agreeing that no human being should be denied such a basic need as relieving themselves when nature calls. Fast food franchises were next put on the firing line, being cited as a major cause of obesity in the metro while denying customers the use of their facilities as soon as they leave the restaurant.

It was the City infrastructure that was dumbfounded by the suggestion. Already dealing with a monumental budget deficit, the Administration cringed at the thought of the maintenance of thousands of Port-O-Sans across the Five Boroughs. Yet the financial ramifications could not be explained to an idealistic community demanding justice for the underprivileged.

Churches, political organizations and humanitarian groups were galvanized by the call to arms, but the churches were at once knocked back on their heels. They had no answer as to why most were locked during the day, and why restroom facilities were not made available to worshippers. The politicians and humanitarians also backed away from that spotlight, and Adolf Hyatt had won the day.

His next gambit was to get word out to the Cells once again. He would require all of them to have every homeless person reach out to at least one other in leaving a water bottle out somewhere for refill. When and if possible, they were to leave a note in or on the bottle: FILL ME.

At the break of dawn, a week after what the *New York Post* gleefully called the Piss Parade, homeless people began leaving their empties at bars and restaurants, public facilities, and most places where they could not go in for a drink of water in the dog days of summer. Hyatt had carefully timed the protest so that it coincided with the trash pickups scheduled for the following day. As a result, plastic bottles were piled atop the mountains of garbage bags in front of businesses across Manhattan. Citizens began taking pictures on their cell phones all over town, and soon the Internet was flooded with images of the homeless' latest campaign.

This was met with renewed enthusiasm by homeless advocates, who immediately attacked the issue as to why most water fountains throughout the City were either shut off, broken, or reduced to such a trickle they were impossible to use. City representatives once again pointed to their budget, stating that they were forced to give priority to basic necessities such as housing, welfare programs and social services. They were unable to sacrifice funds for creature comforts lest one of their more important projects become underfinanced. This evolved into the joke of the day, as cartoonists across the Internet depicted vagrants crawling across sidewalks towards water fountains as desert oases, pleading for a sip of Creature Comfort. Comedians jumped all over it as well, pointing out that the best way to solve the inaccessibility of restroom facilities was to give people no need to use the toilet.

The homeless were suddenly the hot topic throughout the City and across the Internet as Hyatt's tactics began gaining attention around the country. Feedback from his Cells was highly encouraging as they reported vagrants receiving encouragement and more donations by well-meaning citizens. He decided to up the ante by asking all homeless people to sacrifice three dollars from their stashes and buy themselves a cup of coffee at a nice place, preferably with a companion. This would be done on what he would call the Second Day of Defiance.

A little over a week after the newspapers had glorified Messages In A Bottle throughout NYC, homeless people began showing up in hotel lobbies, restaurants and upscale bars and cafes across Manhattan. Most were immediately rebuffed by management workers, insisting that they were not appropriately dressed for service in such places. Others saw it as a hobo scam and ran them off without explanation. Yet others had waitresses at the ready, awaiting the vagrants to finish their coffee so they could swoop in and snatch the cups in exchange for their tabs. Within hours police cars were dispatched throughout the city, accompanied by paddy wagons into which resisters were herded on charges of disorderly conduct.

The American Civil Liberties Union was among one of many civil rights groups who charged into the fray, alleging that the NYPD was depriving the homeless of their rights and discriminating against them as a social class. The Police Department was an old hand at this type of activist harassment, having survived a class action lawsuit back in the 90's filed by panhandlers in Tompkins Square Park. They also weathered a storm in the 00's as officers were accused of arresting the homeless for vagrancy, a law declared unconstitutional in the 1993 decision. Yet they were unprepared for the backlash following the Coffee Clash, as it was dubbed. The NYPD was accused of Gestapo tactics in persecuting the homeless for no other reason than being what they considered undesirables.

It was at that point that Adolf Hyatt made himself known to the public. He proclaimed himself King of the Hoboes on the website, and published a biographical profile showing how he had been homeless since the age of thirteen. He had spent over three decades riding the rails, witnessing firsthand the struggle of the underprivileged and the injustices they suffered at the hands of the middle and upper classes. The New Bourgeoisie, as he called it, complained about glass ceilings, dwindling profits and the rising cost of living while ignoring the millions of Americans who were being banished to the bottomless pit of homelessness. He promised a new day in which America would be forced to lend a helping hand to those in desperate need, or the outstretched hands of the needy would grab on tight and drag the Bourgeoisie down into the New Reality.

Hyatt's catchphrase went viral as A New Reality was analyzed across the Internet. Having self-proclaimed himself as The Resolver, satirists conjured up images of a caped crusader with an 'R' emblazoned on his chest. Many compared his campaign to the New Hope of *Star Wars*, while more than a few depicted him as a Darth Vader with a vast army of clone-like vagrants under his command. Regardless of whether Hyatt's message was embraced or rejected, the fact remained that he had contributed to the homeless dialogue like no one before him.

"You know, the Hobo Community isn't anything like the kind of people Hyatt is starting to attract," Veronika pointed out to Evan as they relaxed at his apartment that evening. She was researching the Internet on the situation shortly after word had gotten out that Captain Willard was planning a police investigation. "There are more than a few thieves, beggars and con artists, but all in all, most of them are all about the Work For Food signs. They distinguish themselves from bums who don't work, and tramps who rarely work."

"Well, you'd better plan on pulling the Bum word out of your vocabulary," Evan teased her. "That's the only term you used to describe them until Chief Madden dropped the hint that you might get upped if you scored on this one."

"I'm not sure that was quite how I put it," she peered over her gold-rimmed glasses at him. "He said that this was an opportunity for advancement, just like any other big case. Plus, I have not been throwing that word Bum all over the place."

"Well, you've been using it a lot more than the mess-around words," he cocked his head towards her. "I haven't been hearing much of that at all lately."

"I'll have you know I'm not just a hole propped up on two legs," she retorted indignantly. "I'm a twenty-seven year old woman, and I'm very concerned about my future. I don't want to be an undercover cop when I'm forty. This might be a major opportunity for me. If I can turn this around for the Department and find a way to close Hyatt down, Madden's going to owe me big-time, and I intend to collect."

"I think all you might end up collecting is that ten inches of black mamba they say he keeps in his drawers," Evan taunted her. "In which case you may be right. You'd better go and get it now, it might not be so hot when it turns forty."

"Yeah?" she turned towards him, opening her robe just enough for him to see her nakedness beneath her robe. "Keep it up and I can guarantee you'll never find out."

"You know," he said, clicking off the hockey telecast and rolling off the couch, "you got a bad habit of disturbing me while I'm watching a game. Now you've got me needing a cold shower."

"Well, you poor underprivileged man, if you make it a warm one, maybe I can make it up to you," she stood up and threw her arms onto his shoulders as he walked over.

"You got a date," he grinned.

They headed for the bathroom, blissfully unaware that it would soon become a luxury they were to sorely miss in a very short time.

Chapter Three

They had been in Chief Madden's office a week earlier, before they put their grievances aside and began sleeping at each other's apartments again. Some of the other teams interviewed for the assignment and the job was still open. According to rumor, the prospective team would have a sitdown with Madden and Captain Willard. If it went okay, the next step would be a written proposal on how the assignment would be handled. From there, Madden and Willard would review the best proposals and make a decision.

Part of the team's magic was how Veronika could dive right in with her vigorous optimism, guaranteeing how the job would get done with lightning precision and prodigious energy in the shortest amount of time. Whenever she stopped to take a breather, Evan would jump in with his facts and statistics, pointing out what they had done previously and were fully capable of doing again. Their goal was driving their target audience to mental exhaustion, and both Madden and Willard had heard enough to make them give the team a crack at it.

"Your job is to infiltrate the Hobo Underground, get inside Adolf Hyatt's infrastructure, and find out everything you can about his insurgent movement. If you can give us enough information for us to indict him and get a conviction, you've earned your gold badge," Police Chief Joel Madden assured her.

"You're going deep undercover, maybe deeper than you can handle," Captain Ty Willard insisted. "This isn't gonna work if you two aren't gonna be able to work together."

"Are you two gonna be able to put your past differences aside in order to get the job done?" Madden asked them.

Evan Carlow tapped his fingers contemplatively on the desk, looking at Madden, then Willard, and finally Veronika before replying.

"I don't foresee any problems. I'd love to see Roni get what she deserves. We're like clockwork out there on the field. You give us the green light, we'll come up with a game plan, tell you what we need, and we'll give you this guy on a silver platter."

"Now that sounds like a vote of confidence," Veronika smiled appreciatively before looking over at Madden and Willard. "I'd call it an offer you can't refuse. Chief, Captain, we've done it before and we can do it again. We've taken down an identity theft ring, an illegal waste disposal racket and a crack posse. Doing up a gang of vagrants'll be a walk in the park."

"This is exactly what's going to blow your cover," Madden stabbed his finger onto the conference table. "I do not see how you're gonna sell your story to those bums, especially Hyatt. These people have lived on the street all their lives, they *are* the street. I don't see how you're gonna be able to pull this off, Heydrich. There's a hundred eyes on every block these days, just like Hyatt says. You're not gonna be able to go back to your loft, you're not gonna be able to shower or change clothes, you're gonna be living on garbage. If you get sick you'll be sitting in a waiting room for hours in a clinic. Woman, you need to think about what you're getting into. Granted, if you win the gold it'll change your career, but if you blow your cover you'll singlehandedly wreck this operation, and that can send your career into reverse."

"Something to think about, Roni," Evan shrugged nonchalantly. "We're in this together. If you come out I come out, and I wouldn't want something like that on my record. It's your call, though. If you think you can pull it off, I'm with you to the finish."

"I want that gold badge," Veronika insisted. "It'll be worth it. I'm all in."

"Okay, people, it's your ball," Madden said. "When I've got your proposal on my desk, I'll go over it with Captain Willard, we'll tweak it up, and we'll have you on the street by Monday."

"Wonder why none of the other teams were pushing too hard for the assignment?" Veronika mused as they headed for the nearby parking garage.

"That's a no-brainer," Evan shook his head. "We're gonna be sleeping in the damn street, girl. It's like they say, the night has a thousand eyes. If any of the homeless folks in Hyatt's network spot us going in and out of our apartments, our cover's blown. It could be anyone: a bag lady, a Work For Food guy, an addict, a drunk. We don't know how Hyatt's earning their allegiance, but we do know that lots of people risked their handouts and even arrest to participate in his 'acts of defiance'. Bottom line, we're living like vagrants until we put together enough intel on Hyatt to make our charges stick."

"Well, now suppose he decides to become the 21st century Henry David Thoreau and sticks to civil disobedience? Suppose he never incites the homeless to a criminal act? How does this work, do we spend three months, six months on the street and don't get a badge?"

"You should have thought of that earlier, lady. Kinda late for that now."

They drove back to Veronika's apartment, deciding that they would spend the night at her place. They would close it down and spend the next couple of days at his place before hitting the streets Monday morning. They would consider it a mini-vacation, a big goodbye to their creature comforts as they entered a world of deprivation where over one hundred thousand New Yorkers existed daily.

Within days, their worst expectations would barely begin to be realized.

Adolf Hyatt's Twelve Disciples had been carefully selected over the years, and remained in the shadows until now as part of his Invisible Network. Most of the elder statesmen of the Hobo Underground had an inkling that his Network existed but never could prove that he was operating outside of the rules of the underground. Due to the fact that his suspected Network had proven so benevolent and stabilizing wherever it appeared, the elders were loath to impeach or depose the reigning King of the Hoboes.

Each of the Disciples earned their membership by holding their own in hand-to-hand combat against the member of Hyatt's choice. From there, they would be required to bring Hyatt $1,000 in forty-eight hours by any means necessary. They were next given an assignment which generally consisted of identity theft that Hyatt would be able to use in a future scam. Finally, they had to bring an attractive woman into the Satanic Circle for a midnight ritual. The only way to leave the Disciples was through death or banishment, and most agreed that the terms were one and the same.

The Twelve who were Hyatt's hardcore crew had all done time for charges ranging from manslaughter to rape, assault, burglary, narcotics, theft and prostitution. They were all capable of using their skills to earn money for Hyatt and the Twelve as the need arose. Yet they delegated those responsibilities to their Follower, who would lead the Believers of their Cell on money runs at Hyatt's behest. The Follower was considered the Rail Dog of the Disciple and was his virtual slave, committed to do his bidding in exchange for protection. An attack against the Follower was an attack on the property of the Disciple. An offense against a Disciple was as an attack on Hyatt himself.

It was the females of the homeless community who paid the highest price when the Network spread into their area. They were treated as go-fers and serfs within Hyatt's fiefdom, forced to carry out errands and participate in scams, and often physically abused. Most of the women were hungry, needed a place to stay, or desired the protection of a crowd. Hyatt knew from experience that homeless women who felt unloved often confused sex with affection, and cherished the arms that held them. Hyatt found that they could often be held far longer than they had originally planned.

Young boys and teenagers were used the same way as the women for the same reasons. The members of the Cell were encouraged to recruit among male children, and most of them took four youngsters under their wing as prescribed. They became as modern-day Fagins, sending the boys out into the streets as thieves, pickpockets and shoplifters. They would bring their scores to the campfire at the end of the day, contributing all to the pot. The pot was split fifty-fifty, and the Cell member divided his share with the Follower while the remaining half was divided among the four boys. It created an intense competition among the boys, as they would vent their anger against one who did not contribute as much yet earned an equal share. The Cell member would encourage beatings of slackers who did not keep up with the pack.

The Hyatt Clan was the antithesis of the homeless community and the Hobo Underground, whose general philosophy was as that of flea market vendors across America. Everyone watched each other's back, for if not, no one would be there to watch theirs. Yet no one could prove that the Clan operated as they did, for no one would dare betray their secrets. Most of the elders of the Hobo Underground had an idea what was going on, but whenever they came to call upon him they found no fault in him. They found him to be a blessing to the community where he stayed, and the locals had nothing but praise for him.

It was the Days of Defiance that caused the Campfires across the Hobo Underground to entreat the Elders of the Four Corners to intercede. The consensus was that Hyatt's civil disobedience could prove harmful to the Underground, especially in conservative rural communities who would not tolerate such activity. Activists in those areas would be quick to incite public opinion against vagrants to the brink of violence. Hyatt would be forced to account for his actions and explain what he had planned, if anything, for the future.

It was three o'clock in the morning when the hoboes gathered around the campfire beneath the Manhattan Bridge. The Elders of the Four Corners had arrived that afternoon. After being met and greeted by local hoboes, they ate, drank and rested before the meeting with Hyatt. They came alone and sat alone with Hyatt, his twelve Disciples guarding the campfire from the shadows. They passed the bottle of port around the campfire between the five of them, and once it was empty the discussion began.

"Adolf, it seems to us that your campaign of defiance has brought unwanted attention upon the larger community of homeless people in New York City, to the benefit of a few concerned with the movement," Boxcar Billy, the Elder of the Northwest, opened the discussion. "Most of the benefit we can see is drawing publicity to yourself. We have seen not one portable toilet set up by the City, or one new or repaired drinking fountain since your protest. On the other hand, many establishments have made their facilities unavailable to homeless people as a rebuke for their acts of defiance."

"I am far from finished," Hyatt insisted. "If they had set up the portable toilets, we would not have demanded water. If they had given us water, my argument would have come to an end. Since they have not given us water, then we will continue to demand to be given the same basic privileges that every other citizen enjoys. Believe me, there is a laundry list of things that we do not have that will be given with their blessings in time."

"Brother Hyatt, if your campaign causes more facilities to be closed to us, and you achieve no success in your protests, are you going to continue at the expense of your fellow vagrants?" Crossroads Clyde, the Elder of the Southwest, squinted at him. "Right now, there are homeless people who spend time in the libraries to get off the streets. Lots of them say your name's gotten pretty big on that Internet. People are starting to think your concern is more about your name than getting a break for fellow travelers."

"There has to be a name for them to put at the top of their list, a head they can chop off," Hyatt insisted. "If I am to be the sacrificial lamb for our community, then so be it. Let the whole world know that Adolf Hyatt is the King of the Hoboes, and I will give my very life for the good of the homeless universe."

"Friend, it is sounding a whole lot like you have given this a lot of thought and you have a careful plan to go about this," Mulligan Mike of the Southeast considered. "We have not come here to tell you what to do, only to express the concerns of the community and ask that you help us reconcile them. Most of the homeless people in New York came here because of the benefits that are available here. Maybe they're not getting egg in their beer, but it's a helluva lot better than what they get in most places down South. If the City of New York turns against them, brother, they will have no place else to go."

"Neither have I come here just to test my skills, then run away. I have come here to fight and give my life, if need be, for this community that has struggled far too long. The blacks have won their rights, the gays have won their rights, but the homeless are still being treated like strangers in the Land of Liberty. That day will end, and I am the Resolver of this social problem!"

"I hate to say this, brother Hyatt, but it seems to us that you are putting yourself ahead of the community, and we have no choice but to sanction you," Midnight Maury declared. "If you do not agree to give up this crusade and leave New York, we will put out the word against you and have you deposed as King of the Hoboes."

"And I say to you that you no longer exist!" Hyatt stood in righteous indignation. "The Elders of the Four Corners will now be called the Elders of the Four Winds! You will shrivel and blow away, and from now on you are just a myth, a rumor! From now on you no longer exist!"

With that, a number of the Disciples rushed forth from the shadows and drove knives into the backs of the Elders. They stabbed them to death, then wrapped their bodies in garbage bags which were also filled with rocks. They taped them up tightly, then carried them to the concrete walls along the riverside and dropped them into the East River. The Hyatt Clan then disappeared into the night, with no trace of the Elders ever to be found.

Unknown to anyone, a lone young man had been lurking in the shadows, witnessing the entire event. He had been sleeping in the bushes since nightfall, and thought nothing of the activity until the campfire was lit and the discussion began in earnest. Khalid Sangani watched the killing in horror, realizing that detection would cost his life. He remained frozen in place until the Clan had left, then fled with his dark secret into the night.

Veronika and Evan decided to spend their last night at his place indulging their fantasies. She went to Victoria's Secret and purchased exquisite black silk lingerie which included a nippleless bra, crotchless panties, a garter belt and seamed nylons. She picked out a $200 black satin dress and heels, and it was all Evan could do to keep his hands off her before they left the apartment.

They headed out to Keens Steakhouse on West 36th Street, its turn-of-the-century ambiance always scintillating with their framed memorabilia and world-famous pipe collections from the Pipe Club of eras long since past. Veronika ordered the house specialty mutton chop, while Evan went for the Maine lobster and filet mignon. They had a bottle of Chianti to go with their order, and they were fully satisfied after paying their tab and cruising back to the apartment.

Evan dimmed the lights and put on some soft music. Veronika poured them some more Chianti before standing at the sliding glass patio door with her back to him. She swayed softly in time to the romantic pop melody, and she took him past the limits of his self-control. Her long blonde hair was as a thick veil across her back, and her hips and thighs swelled beneath the silken dress. He walked up behind her and put his arms around her waist, and she arched backwards so that her hips pressed against his groin. She put down her glass as he turned her around and lowered her to the alpaca rug on the carpeted floor.

He pulled down the straps of her dress, feasting on the ripe berries of her breasts as she wriggled free of her garment. He began tearing off his own clothes as he crawled backwards, down to her crotch where he ripped her panties away and thrust his face between her legs. She gasped with passion as he began nibbling at her body, causing her to writhe so that he could endure no more. He pounced upon her and drove himself deep inside her, and she moaned and bucked beneath him until they exploded into ecstasy within minutes.

"You sure you want to go through with this?" Evan held her close as they lay exhausted on the carpet.

"It's what I want more than anything beside you."

"That's good enough for me," he hugged her tight as they cuddled for a long time afterwards.

They would both look back and consider the fact that the rug on the carpeted floor, in and of itself, was one of the least of the luxuries they would surrender in exchange for the challenge of their careers and their lives.

Chapter Four

Veronika was walking along the Bowery at the crack of dawn that Monday morning dressed in a worn blue hoodie, a black T-shirt and jeans, and black steel-tip shoes. She had her hair tied back in a bun, and it was getting frizzy since she went without washing it over the weekend. She didn't have any makeup, clipped her nails and removed her polish. She had gone frowsy when they infiltrated the hacker ring, but this was different. She had a plastic comb and five dollars to her name. The reality of what she had gotten herself into was sinking in with every step, and she knew that this was truly what could be termed as paying one's dues.

Being a police officer was, in a lot of ways, like being part of the biggest gang in the City. When one was wearing their badge or in uniform, no one dared look crooked at them. Some did, but not for long. Ever since the Giuliani Era and 9/11, the NYPD ruled the streets with all the force of Homeland Security behind them. All the losers and abusers of the underworld could do was operate in the shadows when and where the NYPD did not see them.

Now Veronika was on the street, and would be working in the shadows. She was, for all intents and purposes, out of contact with Evan and the rest of the force. She would have to eat at the food banks and the soup kitchens, and make it to the shelters before nightfall or she would be sleeping in the street. The scariest part about this was not carrying her pistol. She was packed during the sting operation against the MS-13 drug dealers, and she was carrying during the operation against the hacker ring. Without a purse and dressing in threadbare clothes, she had no place for her Glock-17. There had been few times throughout her eight-year career that she had gone unarmed, and it had her feeling very vulnerable.

She walked down to East Seventh Street and made her way towards Alphabet City. It was not the danger zone it had been two decades ago, but was still not one of the safer places to walk around in Lower Manhattan. She could not remember the last time she had been down here. It was most likely back when she was riding around in a patrol car, back when Chief Madden laid eyes on her and thought such a beautiful cop should not be walking the beat. He had been her guardian angel for most of her career, but right now she was light years from the pearly gates.

"Hey, you," the whooping sound of a police siren nearly made her jump. She turned around and saw that a patrol car had cruised up behind her. It was a couple of young cops, and she was quite sure they were not here to offer support.

"Yeah?" she asked testily, and they did not like the tone of her voice. They switched on their strobe lights and got out of the car, heading straight towards her.

"You looking to score?" the driver smirked. "Let's see some ID."

"What the hell are you talking about?" Veronika was not in a good mood. "I'm just taking a walk, it's a free country."

"Not for hookers," he grabbed her arm and led her towards the hood of the car. "You're not hooking, are you?"

"Do I look like I'm dressed for hooking?"

"Do the faggots on Christopher Street dress to go hooking? Let's see some ID, I'm not gonna ask you again."

"I left it at home," she said as they turned her around and made her prop her hands on the hood.

"Where do you live?"

"At the shelter."

"Which shelter?"

"Whichever shelter's got room."

"All right, you're going downtown," the other cop pulled out his cuffs and locked her wrists behind her back.

"For what?" she demanded. "This is bullshit!"

"Vagrancy," the cop opened the door and shoved her head down, forcing her into the back seat.

"There is no more law against vagrancy!" she snapped at them as they got back in the car.

"Tell it to the magistrate," the driver popped a stick of gum in his mouth as he gunned the engine. She had not been on the street for two hours and was already on her way downtown.

They drove her to Manhattan Central Booking on Centre Street where she was placed in a holding cell. It was packed with drunks, drug addicts, whores, child abusers and shoplifters. She was pissed off by the time she was taken to the booking desk and fingerprinted, and a couple of the bigger policewomen came by in case she turned rowdy.

"Name?"

"Ronnie Hyde."

"Age? Weight? Okay, go on over there and they'll get your prints and take your picture."

"What'd they pick you up for?" they rolled each ink-stained finger across a card.

"No reason whatsoever. I didn't do shit."

"Okay, well, we'll be checking on that. You'll be able to see the magistrate when you're called."

They brought her in turn to a darkly lit area that reminded her of the old Nazi movies where they took prisoners to SS interrogators before they were tortured. They brought her up to a bespectacled, middle-aged fellow who she knew wasn't giving her any breaks here.

"Okay, they arrested you for vagrancy and loitering. Are you able to afford a lawyer or pay your bail?"

"I'm not paying a damn thing. I didn't do anything."

"I don't want to hold you in contempt, so calm down, ma'am. You have a right to make a phone call before they assign you to a cell. The City Attorney will review your case, and they'll decide whether you can be released on your own recognizance. Next."

By the time she was placed in a cell with four other women who already had the bunks, she was fit to be tied. She had an inkling that many of the people in this business were in it due to their low-average intelligence, but now she was certain. She had never met so many stupid people in her life, and the idiots who arrested her were the brightest of them all. She could only hope that whatever moron was processing her prints would see who she was and pull her out of here. She sat down beside the seatless toilet near the door, closing her eyes and hoping to snooze so as not to endure any of these losers trying to talk to her.

"Hyde? Ronnie Hyde?" a guard came by about an hour later.

"Ooh, richy bitchy, she gots a lawyer," an obese Puerto Rican woman teased from her cot. "*Hasta la vista*, baby."

"Shut your hole, you fat bitch, or I'll kick your teeth out of your face," Veronika snapped.

"Wha-at?" the woman propped herself up on an elbow.

"C'mon, Hyde, get a move on," the guard insisted.

"I'll see you again," the fat woman warned her before rolling back over.

"You better hope not, you porky pig," Veronika retorted before the cell door was locked behind her. She began along a long walk through a maze of hallways, and she appreciated the fact that if one were to slip away from their guard, it would be nearly impossible to find one's way out. She also knew that if they were not going to let her out, she would have to trade her rag-assed clothes for orange pajamas and be forced to sleep on the floor for the night. Even though she kept thinking of that gold badge and the $90k salary, this gig was really starting to suck.

They brought her into what she knew was an interrogation room with the big two-way mirrors and three cops standing around outside. She sauntered in and dropped into a seat, staring moodily at the mirrors wondering what dumbasses might be staring back. After about ten minutes, the door to the room was opened and another vagrant was herded in by two cops. She wondered what all these cops were doing here instead of the screws. Most likely, like the dipshits who picked her up, they had nothing better to do.

"Well, we just wanted you to know you're not alone out there," the husky black man took off his ski cap and rubbed his scalp briskly as he sat in a chair by the door.

"Captain Willard!" Veronika was astounded.

"Last chance, Heydrich," he stared across at her. "The only thing left for you is sleeping under a bridge. You gonna be able to handle it?"

"I'm going for the gold," she gazed intently into his eyes. "I'm going inside, I'm gonna get down right beside Hyatt, and when I've got enough to hold him I'm gonna take him. Did you actually go through all this just to ask me that?"

"No, I came in the back way, same way I'm going out," Willard said airily. "Everybody saw you come in through the prisoners' entrance. You got printed, appeared before the magistrate, sat in a cell, and that was after you got picked up on Avenue A. You got your street creds, so you're good to go."

"So I can go?"

"They're letting you out and Carlow's gonna be tailing you, but don't go depending on i.e. don't want you two being seen hanging out together, it'd be too easy for you to get made. He'll stay on you as much as possible and we'll have patrol cars looking for you. But again, don't depend on it."

"Gotcha."

The guards opened the door and let him out, and for the first time she felt truly alone.

On the first night, she headed up to Central Park and decided that she was far better off dozing in the bushes rather than on a bench where either police or gangsters could mess with her. She walked along the footpath for over a mile before she spotted a treeline surrounded by foliage near the Jacqueline Onassis Reservoir. She furtively crept across the grass, looking around for signs of cops, and slipped into the bushes without incident. She only hoped there were no insects in the place of her choice, and sat down in a clear space to test the ground. She had been walking all day, and her feet were throbbing as she finally was able to stretch out.

She dropped back and stared straight up at the starry sky, feeling a strange sense of comfort for the first time. It was if the sky was a great canopy streaked with stars that were as diamonds as far as the eye could see. At once she missed Evan terribly and wished he was here with her. Maybe he was out there, on a bench keeping an eye on her as she slept. She had been on the street all day since sunrise, stopping occasionally to rest her feet, and she was sure he was trailing her. She found comfort in the thought and eventually went to sleep.

When she woke up the next morning, she was nearly hit by a panic attack. She realized she could not change her socks or underwear, much less her shirt or pants. She could not brush her teeth, take a shower or even use the restroom. This was a desperate situation and she had to sort it out. She decided to find a Starbucks and buy coffee in order to use the restroom and wash up. It was going to wipe out half of the five dollars she had with her, and that meant she was going to have to find a soup kitchen and a shelter if she was going to make it through Day Two.

She walked past a couple of Starbucks shops and managed to restrain herself. She thought twice about busting herself out for one cup of coffee, and decided to scope the terrain and see what was out here. She had immersed herself in thought most of yesterday, which had become a self-pitying blur. Today she had to get situated and find out where she could go to sort herself out.

"Say, guy," she called out to a Work For Food bum who looked as if the corner of 28th Street and Sixth Avenue was his permanent residence. If Godzilla came through here and shit fire on the intersection, destroying every man and beast, this man would have returned to his corner the following day. "You know where they're serving lunch?"

"Three blocks down, the Holy Apostles," said the man who never smiled despite the amiable tone of his voice. "They start serving at 10:30, if you get in line now you'll be able to find a seat and get back in line for seconds before they close."

She thanked him graciously before making a beeline down the street, then nearly laughed out loud at her predicament. She had to pee so bad she was ready to bust, and she imagined there were germs marching up and down her panties and socks. She felt as if her tongue had swollen from thirst, and thought her feet had grown a half size overnight. She resolved that if Chief Madden did not give her a detective badge after this, she would put a gun in his mouth.

She saw a dozen people in line to the entrance of the food kitchen inside the venerated cathedral. She got in line and squeezed her legs together, praying her bladder would hold out until the doors open. She saw a homeless woman sitting crosslegged on the concrete and followed suit, finding it easier to endure the need to pee. She tried dozing off again, and it made the time drift by until the dining room finally opened to the public.

Veronika scurried off to the bathroom and took a blessed leak before filling both of her back pockets with paper towels. She decided she would come back here before leaving to wash her socks and panties, taking a quick whore's bath before going back to get in line. She was astonished when a man who looked as if he had not eaten in days insisted she get in line ahead of him. She thanked him profusely as she picked up a tray laden with food handed to her by a smiling volunteer.

She had not eaten for an entire day, and the turkey, ham and pasta casserole was every bit as heavenly as the mutton chop she had at Kerns just four days ago. The broccoli was equally as divine, and she savored her buttered roll before eating her sliced peaches bit by bit. The iced tea was as champagne, and when she was done her little tummy was fit to bust. She saw some of the people getting back in line, but it was getting crowded with vagrants and she could stand no more. She went back to the restroom and pulled off her socks and panties, washing them in the sink before sticking them in her hoodie pocket and heading back to the street.

She made it a point to take two five-mile jogs each week, but it was not the same as walking the pavement all day. After her run, she could go home and take a hot bubble bath. Out here, all she had to look forward to was a park bench to sit on. She walked down to Washington Square Park, then found out about the Olivieri Drop-In Center on 30th Street near 7th Avenue. She was able to take a shower and have dinner before asking if she could stay overnight.

"Ain't no place to stay unless you got a kid or have your old man beat you bloody," a middle-aged black woman told her. "All the shelters for men. If a woman needs one they puts you on a list, and when your name comes up you gots to stay there as long as you can. Once you leaves, you off the list and gots to start over. Ain't no place for a homeless woman, honey. You best get yourself cleaned up and finds yourself a man."

The sun began setting on her second night on the street as she headed back to Central Park, having a strange sense of pride in having her own little spot in the bushes where she could stay for free, with no one telling her what to do or when she had to leave. She tried to forget about the fact that she would have to make it back to the Church of the Holy Apostles tomorrow morning and the Olivieri Center that afternoon if she wanted to wash her underwear and avoid swooning over from hunger.

She literally turned the corner on the third night when she decided to camp out in the IRT train station on 14th Street at Union Square. She knew that if she found a section of newspaper and folded it up as if reading it, she could catch some REM sleep while pretending to wait for a train. If a cop came along, he might think she had dozed off and leave her alone. She spent one of the five dollars she had bummed at a stoplight that morning (*"Hey, I'll give you a twenty if you take a ride with me!"*) to buy a token and take her chances. She lucked out in finding a freshly-discarded *New York Times* sticking out of the top of a trash barrel, and decided to take the whole paper along with her. She found that the bench at the top of the platform was vacant, and yawned and stretched in noticing the whole station seemed empty.

The Number Five train rumbled in, and she watched a couple of grim-faced clerks and a frazzled-looking waitress get off. They trudged towards the exit as the train roared away down the tunnel, leaving scraps of paper flying around on the track in its wake. She managed to doze off again, but perceived movement along the stairs and rubbed her eyes. A cop appeared on the platform, glancing over at her as she made a show of shaking the paper to smooth the page she was reading. He strolled off down to the other edge of the platform, and she leaned back and closed her eyes again.

She watched a middle-aged vagrant shuffling to the beat of the living dead, his vacant gaze looking down the platform as he stood at the edge for a few minutes. He finally turned and resumed his mechanical walk, his rucksack hanging as a koala cub as he meandered towards the tunnel and walked down the steps. Veronika watched in fascination as he disappeared in the shadows as if he worked there.

Following a hunch, she got up from the bench and made her way to the end of the platform as if looking for her train. She casually glanced down the other end of the tunnel and saw that the vagabond had disappeared. She tentatively strolled down to the edge of the platform and saw the grimy cement steps leading to a pathway running alongside the tracks to the left, and a series of archways leading off to adjoining tunnels to the right. Veronica looked about carefully before trotting down the steps.

She was careful as a deer, looking right and left before taking each step. If she had been on the field in a standard role she would have her pistol drawn and at the ready. She made her way to the first archway and assumed that was where the vagrant had gone. She ducked inside and saw it was dimly illuminated by a 40-watt bulb. She stepped inside and marveled at the fact that, outside of the cake of dust and grime that had accumulated over decades, it was remarkably barren.

She saw another passageway along the far wall of the 10x10 area and crept across the concrete floor, peeking inside. She detected motion and knew that if it was workers she would have to haul ass, probably out of the station and back onto the street lest they call the police.

She peeked around the wall and was astonished by the sight before her eyes. It appeared that she had finally made her first break in the case at last.

"They have an entire encampment of their own down in the subway tunnels," Veronika was fervent as she gave her report to Lieutenant Shreve in the interview room at Manhattan Central Booking the next morning. "There's got to be as many as twenty people down there. They even cook down there over cans of Sterno. I met people, they told me a ton of stuff about the way the underground community works and who goes where, who does what. The big thing is, I found out where the Hyatts hang out and how I might be able to get inside."

She had returned to Avenue A and East 7th Street at dawn and loitered until the same patrol car that picked her up on Day One came cruising along. She told them she needed to be taken in to speak to Captain Willard and kicked the car door for emphasis. They hopped out of the car and slapped the cuffs on, then tossed her in the rear and took her over to Centre Street. She went through the routine but found they had sent Shreve dressed as a bum instead.

"Okay, if we're able to keep this going without you getting yourself killed, I think we can put together a case and make it stick," Shreve decided. He was a good-natured desk jockey who expedited Willard's paperwork and made himself indispensable on the office level. He was a nine-to-fiver who intensely disliked these types of assignments. All he wanted to do was get Veronika's report back to Police Plaza.

"I'm making some good connections, and I'm meeting some major movers and shakers," she insisted. "I'm learning lots of names, I'm learning the vernacular, I'm learning the way things work on the street. I'm telling you, Lieutenant, you have no idea what a complicated tier structure they have. The homeless people we see on the street are the visible tip of the iceberg. This is a stratified, highly organized society, and if Hyatt is able to unite them into a militant movement, they have the capability of dragging this city into a state of anarchy and chaos."

"All right, I'll get together with Captain Willard and let him in on the details," Shreve relented, rubbing his eyes wearily. "Carlow's been reporting nightly and he's keeping close watch on you. He saw you go into the IRT station last night, and he says you've been holing up in the bushes at Central Park the night before. Just think of him as a cell phone. In some of the places you go, it'll be like having no signal, so proceed with caution."

"Gotcha."

"In future, if you've got something for us, shoot us an e-mail. I know it probably does you a lot of good to make physical contact with us, but we can't keep coming down here and going through the funnel to meet with you. Plus, the bums in Alphabet City are gonna make you if they see you getting a ride downtown upon request. Carlow's your lifeline if we need to get in touch. Use your e-mail to keep us updated. We appreciate the input, keep us posted."

Veronika watched the guards escort Shreve out of the room, realizing that her voyage had truly begun and she had just drifted far, far away from shore.

Chapter Five

"This is what I have come to warn you about! This is the appointed time for me to have come here to open your eyes to what they are doing to you! Here I stand, and here I can show you right before your eyes what they are doing for themselves at your expense!"

Adolf Hyatt wore a black fedora and trench coat, the wind rustling his clothes as he stood on a stack of plywood amidst a crowd of over a hundred homeless people gathered around him that spring morning. His eyes were blazing with righteous indignation and his voice quavered with anger as if those he railed against were standing there before him.

Veronika Heydrich watched him with a strange sense of admiration tempered by her sense of duty. It was the feeling one gets when watching any great leader, like the leader of the MS-13 crack gang, the boss of the toxic dumping crew, the guru geek of the hacker ring. You appreciated the talent of the worthy opponent before you took them down.

"These Hudson Yards have not only been a railroad supply depot since this city was created, but it has been a haven for the Hobo Underground, for runaway kids, for homeless people all over Manhattan. No one who came here was ever turned away, no one ever approached a campfire without being offered a bite of what there was to eat or a sip of what there was to drink. No one who laid their head to rest here worried about whether they were going to get robbed or beat up or killed. This was, and has always been, our community. Now the rich people are going to tear it down, and in its place will be built another condominium, another residential sector, another complex. This will be another place where only the rich will be allowed to live. This will be another place where you are unwanted. This is another place where you will be forbidden under penalty of law!"

The picture was coming together, but it wasn't a case of her vision having improved. This was something that was happening before her very eyes. She was surrounded by the kind of people she had stood in line with at the soup kitchens, the women she waited with at the Olivieri for a chance to take a shower, the men she slept alongside in the IRT station despite the deafening roar of a passing train every twenty minutes. These were the people living hand to mouth, day to day, hoping they could find a place to grab a meal, use the restroom, a corner to sleep in. These were the homeless, many of them hopeless. Hyatt was up there speaking everything in their hearts they saw no use in saying.

"People are occupying Wall Street because they feel they are being cheated and robbed? I say *we* occupy the Hudson Yards because we *are* being cheated and robbed! If we stand by and watch them dig this yard up and replace it with their ivory towers, where will we go next? They no longer have any space for us at their shelters, they can't stand the sight of us on their streets, and the day will come when they will rout us from their subways. Their ultimate goal is to eradicate you from the streets of New York, and if you do not take a stand here, soon there will be nowhere left for you to stand!"

It reminded her of an old Roberta Flack song as he turned in her direction, his blazing blue eyes staring into the crowd. At once she felt as if he was staring straight at her, and his words seemed to be directed at her, cutting into her heart.

"They place their children on pedestals, and their women on their mantelpieces as their trophies. Yet they have no place for our women and children! Since they do not have the resources to guarantee security in a co-ed sleeping environment, they allow the use of their facilities to the man and turn the women away. Children are turned over to the police, where they are returned to the abusive homes they escaped from, or sent to juvenile halls where they are gang-raped by older inmates. There are three facilities in New York City for all of its homeless women, and they are spread across three boroughs. Where do all these women go? Where can they feel safe and protected? Word around the campfire was that you could always go to the Hudson Yards where the hoboes would protect you. Women and children, if you do not stand beside us now, the Hudson Yards will be no more!"

"He's telling the truth," a voice behind her said. "If we don't stand together, we will all starve alone by ourselves."

She turned around and beheld a young boy of sixteen, about 5'4" and one hundred twenty pounds. He was East Indian, with glossy jet-black hair, copper-colored skin, onyx eyes and dark borders around his thick lips. He wore a gray hoodie and t-shirt with tattered black jeans and generic black sneakers, looking very much like he had cut classes for the day.

"Yeah, so what's the game plan, is he gonna pull a Gandhi and have us lay down on the construction sites until the cops carry us off? I've been downtown twice this week. If I get taken in again they'll probably ship me off to Attica."

"Where you been staying?"

"Why do you want to know?"

"Okay, you found a good hiding place. I had one, but something real bad happened there, and I'm on the move again. I just thought you had a place I could hang out at."

"I am the Resolver!" Hyatt exhorted the crowd. "I will bring resolution to all your concerns, all your problems, all your worries and all your cares! They call me King of the Hoboes, yet I am but one of you, one who would gladly lay down my life for the rest of you. If you go to them for food and drink, they will turn you away, but I will walk with you until we find what you need. If you go to them for a place of rest, you will be rejected, but I will stay with you until you find rest and I will watch over you."

"Can you help me get in with those guys? Can you get me close to Hyatt?"

"You know the old saying about moths," he was cryptic. "You may be attracted by the light and warmth of the flame, but if you get too close, you may be consumed by it."

"I'm willing to take that chance."

"Why?"

"I was doing okay in that world he's talking about," she went into her act. She knew that now was the moment of reckoning in this stage of the operation. When you sold your con it had to be perfect. Someone like Khalid would put it out on the street, and everyone would be able to inspect it for holes. She had to sell him so he would sell it to everyone else who asked about it. "I had a good job, was making money, had a future. Only one day I woke up and realized I wasn't living my life, I was living what everyone else was planning for me. I decided to walk away, to live my own life, to see the world. I wasn't going to let my parents, my bosses, my family and friends decide how my life was gonna turn out. Right now I'm learning what it means to be free. The only thing is, it's like Hyatt is saying. In this world you need protection. You have to have someone watching your back or the wolves will take you down and eat you alive."

"That may be," Khalid looked at her. "But have you considered the fact that you may be trading one master for another? Granted, as Hyatt says, the good shepherd may indeed lay his life down his life for his sheep, but in the end the shepherd is the master of his flock. He would break the legs of a wandering sheep to make sure it never goes astray."

"That may be better than getting sent to Attica," she smirked.

"Tomorrow will begin the Day of Defiance against those who would drive us away from our oasis," Hyatt concluded as he saw the light of hope shining in the eyes of his audience. "Tomorrow we will meet here again on this very spot and join together to defend our resting place from the oppressors! If they wish to take this away from us, then they will take us away one by one until they find us another place of rest!"

"Sounds like game on to me," Veronika watched as Hyatt jumped down from the stack of plywood into his entourage of black-clad Disciples, the crowd slowly drifting away. "I wonder if he's got his Internet thing going with this?"

"You've seen him on the Internet?" Khalid marveled. "Where are you getting access?"

"People can get online at the library, you know."

"What library are you going to? Are you skipping the food line to get computer time?"

"I'm not giving up all my stuff to you. I don't even know your name."

"I'm Khalid," he extended his hand and she gave him an uncharacteristically limp shake.

"I'm Roni. Sounds like you know the town pretty good. You wanna help me get up close to the Hyatts?"

"Right now I'm trying to score some bucks. If you come with me over to the Lior Malka and wait outside, I might be able to pick up enough for us to get a nice dinner."

"You gotta be kidding," he scoffed. She had her hair and nails done at the upscale beauty parlor a few times, and though it was moderately priced, they would probably kick this kid out on his ass.

"Come on," he entreated her. She decided to play this out because she needed an ally, even one as spindly as this. Besides, she knew Evan was out there somewhere, and he would probably put a trace on the kid and have him tagged within the next twenty-four hours.

"Yeah, okay," she relented, and they began the long walk from Chelsea back down towards the Garment District.

She asked him where he came from, and he explained that he ran away from his wealthy parents' home on the Jersey Shore. She was vaguely familiar with Hinduism, having gone through the spiritual journey of adolescence in seeking the truth of life. Although it left her as an agnostic, she remembered enough to be able to carry on a conversation with the best of them. She asked about his family's caste, and he informed her that they were considered among the Vaishya[1].

"This is my blessing in life," he smiled. "I love to sell, and I have an excellent product."

"Yeah? And what's that?"

"This," he touched himself proudly. "It is twelve inches long."

"Hold on. You gotta be kidding. You're going in to the Lior Malka to turn a trick?"

"I can get anywhere from fifty to a hundred dollars for up to an hour. The older ladies pay the most."

"This I have got to see," she shook her head.

They continued along the Avenue of the Americas and turned down West 23rd Street, and Veronika was highly amused by the attitude of the pedestrians. When she was dressed to the max, or out jogging, lots of the men had big smiles on their faces when she passed by. In this frowsy state, they ranged from disapproving frowns to looks of disdain. She reconciled herself to the fact that her cover was foolproof.

Khalid asked her to wait across the street while he went inside. She realized that he was getting over on retired women or housewives at this time of day, and most likely knew a couple of the hairdressers on that shift. She began window-shopping along the street, peering up and down the block to see if she might spot Evan. She knew he was a first-class surveillance pro, and most would have the chance of making him as a snowball in hell.

---

1. merchant class

It just bothered her that she was feeling so vulnerable out here and did not even have the opportunity of reaching out to him. Yet she understood the psychology at work here. Undoubtedly the uncertainty would be showing on her face, which would give anyone the impression that she was someone down on their luck. She studied her countenance in the store windows, and could see a major difference in her unmade face. Though she was a natural beauty, she was not drop-dead gorgeous without her makeup. She resisted feeling sorry for herself, but at times like these it was hard indeed.

Gold badge...gold badge...gold badge.

She saw on a clock in one of the store windows that it was almost ten, and did not plan to miss lunch while Khalid was waiting to stuff his sausage into some old hag. She figured she would wait ten more minutes before heading off to the Holy Apostles. She might come back through here later, or then again, maybe not. She had worked the streets long enough to know that dead leads were almost always better off that way

She got in line at the soup kitchen, then walked up to the Mid-Manhattan Library on 40th Street. It was not very far from Central Park, where she knew she would end up staying under the bushes yet another night. She knew most of the street people left their bedding where they normally slept, but she never saw the sense in that. She remembered seeing the sleeping bags piled beneath underpasses throughout town when she went jogging, and always considered how some mean kids could run over and pee on them when the bums were away.

Once again the computer kiosks were all taken or reserved, and she decided to hang out and read the paper to kill time. She noticed the weary glances of the security guards around the halls, used to the sight of bums coming in to get off the street. The only thing they had to look out for was kids stealing material or cell phones blasting off. She took comfort in knowing if she walked in a month from now, they would be tripping over themselves to kiss her ass.

She killed a couple of hours at the library, imagining that Evan was outside watching and waiting for her to leave. She went over to one of the small ten-minute limit PC's and jumped onto Yahoo, sending him a 'love u Roni' e-mail. She was mildly disappointed that she had not gotten one from him, but realized he was existing under the same conditions as she was. Plus the fact that if he was watching her back, he would not have the luxury of running over to the library and dropping her a line.

She next got the bright idea of going over to Berkeley College on East 43rd Street. If she wandered around the campus she would probably find a place to crash for a bit. All this walking was getting to her, and she would have to hit an intersection and bum money for Dr. Scholl's foot pads sometime tomorrow.

She had not showered today, and having not made a priority of it bothered her more than anything. Between checking out Hyatt's rally and coming across Khalid and checking out his con, plus all the walking, it completely slipped her mind. She got to wash up at the library, but that wasn't making up for not having a change of clothing. It was getting close to rush hour by now, and she would probably be better off finding an intersection and bumming a couple of bucks for Mc Donald's. She would make the Olivieri Center a priority tomorrow, and she would also have to find a Salvation Army and see about getting some extra clothes. That meant she would be walking around with a bag of used clothes all day. This was beginning to suck.

She tried to wrap her head around it as best she could. If she panhandled for a while after lunch, she could probably put enough together to buy a travel bag at the thrift shop. She could then keep a change of clothes in there, probably a T-shirt and sweat pants or leotards, even socks. A toothbrush and toothpaste, soap and basic necessities would work fine. If she was able to find a good place to hide the bag, then she wouldn't have to haul it around all day. She could even stick a loaf of sliced bread in there for snacks.

Now you're thinking on your feet, girl. We're gonna make it after all.

She felt a whole lot better with her game plan and began wandering back up towards Times Square to see the sights. The bright side of this was that she was getting a chance to stop and smell the roses, seeing lots of things she had not the time or patience to check out before. She saw a cool-looking New York City t-shirt she planned to come back for, along with a *Phantom of the Opera* t-shirt. She was also going to make Evan bring her to a play when this was over. They usually hung out around the Village and SoHo, occasionally cruising down to the Wall Street area. Chinatown and Little Italy were off-limits because they didn't want gang members to remember their faces on the field. It made her all the more aware of the restrictions and limits that their jobs carried along with them.

She grew distracted enough by her wanderings to not have noticed the gang of punks that had been tailing her. There were about five of them, possibly Dominicans, and they probably figured that they might be able to take advantage of a homeless woman once it got dark out. They might have had some drugs to offer, a place to sleep, something to eat in exchange for a quickie. If Evan was watching, he would probably have to wait until the last minute before stepping in. If he wasn't watching, she would be in some deep shit without even a knife to protect herself with. Her best chance was to zig-zag towards the Park to lose them. If she went up to a cop he might start some shit and have her hauled back downtown. It would look way too suspicious to a street person in the can who might see her walking in and out three times in one week. She was just going to have to work this out herself.

She was almost looking at this through the eyes of a disinterested person as she hurried down 44th Street towards Fifth Avenue, then north towards Columbus Circle. She considered how a truly homeless woman would have to cope in this type of environment. For the gangsters, it must have been like stalking a deer. They had all the time in the world to work their way along the shadows and side-streets, turning it into a game to see how long they could follow a girl and catch her in a deserted area. It was the thrill of the hunt, and when they caught up with their frightened prey, the offer of protection and creature comfort would prove irresistible to a homeless female.

Crossing one street after another, she caught each light regardless if it put her on a side of the street she had just come from. She figured it would make it easier to spot one or two gangsters jaywalking to keep up, but she did not see that happening. She decided to break into a jog for the last few blocks, which would put some distance between them as well as allow her to see someone running to catch up. She finally made it to 59th Street, and kept jogging into the park before finally stopping to take a breather.

Walking towards the reservoir, she noticed there were far fewer joggers at this time of night than one normally saw during the day. There were no cops out here, just as it was since she started coming out here the last couple of nights. She marveled at the fact that the gangs were not all over the place, though it was more than likely that a call from a rich lawyer strolling about would bring the cops in swarms. She considered the fact that once this was over, she might become a bit more socially active in having the City take a closer look at what homeless women were facing out here.

She felt them before she saw them, a couple of the gangsters trotting on the other side of the grassy field about thirty yards across from her. There were also a couple of figures running on the sidewalk outside the park, but it was impossible to tell if they were exercising or not until they veered back through the bushes onto the grass.

"Say, lady, you know what time it is?"

She turned to face a lone Dominican behind her, and he had a mischievous look on his face as if he was about to let her in on the joke. She glanced behind her and noticed the joggers up ahead watching her, with the two across the field leisurely walking across in their direction. They had followed her for over twenty blocks, and they must have been pretty sure they were going to get what they were looking for.

"Nope, sorry, no watch. I'm waiting on my boyfriend, he's holding it for me."

"He sure picked a weird time and place to come meet you," the kid grinned.

"As you see it," she shrugged.

"Hey Julio, whuzup?" one of the gangsters called as they sauntered down towards Veronika. "What you doing down here? Who's that pretty lady friend of yours?"

"I just met her right here, homes," Julio replied.

"I just picked up some brews, I got them over there in my bag by the grass. I just called Pablito, he's coming across the field right now. Why don't you and the lady come over and pop a top with us?"

"Hey, I already told your friend I'm waiting on someone," she said as the two gangsters to her right drew closer. "You might wanna watch out for the cops before you open any beers. I saw a couple of guys get a ticket a little while ago."

"Girl, you must be Wonder Woman," one of the Dominicans chortled. "I thought I saw you down on Times Square a little while ago. How you get from here to there and back up here so fast?"

"Training for the Olympics," she replied, cutting through the bushes in a shortcut to the sidewalk outside the park. "Have a good one."

"Where you going, baby?" Julio hustled to catch up. "You out here all alone, nowhere to go, you come hang out with us and we got your back."

"Hey, Roni, whuzup. You got static?"

Her heart leaped as she recognized the voice of Khalid coming towards her from the sidewalk. He emerged from the darkness with a reckless swagger that undoubtedly was raising the hackles of the gangsters as he approached.

"Man, I hope that ain't your boyfriend," Julio shook his head.

"Whassamatta, you got a problem with that?" Khalid stopped ten feet away from Julio and Veronika as the other four gangsters closed in.

"Why, you gonna give me a problem?" Julio insisted. At once Khalid reached behind his back, and the gangsters froze in their tracks.

"You gonna throw down?" one asked.

"You gonna make me throw down?" Khalid challenged them.

At once the tension was exacerbated by the whooping of a patrol car siren. A halogen spotlight was thrown in their direction as everyone froze in place.

"Everybody stay where you are!" a loudspeaker squawked.

At once the gangsters took off running northwards into the shadows, splitting up as they hit the bushes.

"C'mon, let's get out of here!" Khalid tugged her arm as he started in the opposite direction. "They're going after those guys!"

They ran eastward along the grass, sprinting across the field through the bushes until they reached the oval walkway leading north towards the reservoir. Satisfied that the police were focused on picking up the Dominicans, they slowed to a walk as Khalid stepped into pace alongside Veronika.

"Where'd you come from?" she wondered. "How'd you find me?"

"I had a hunch you'd be around here, since you were planning to be at the Hudson Yards in the morning. I thought you were gonna wait for me. One of the hairdressers took me in the back, and I made fifty bucks for giving him head."

"Omigod," she exhaled.

"So you camping out around here? I can stay by you and watch your back."

"How do I know I can trust you?"

"I just ran out there pretending I had a piece to help you out," Khalid was exasperated. "Doesn't that count for something?"

"Well, as long as you're not looking for payback," she said, sitting down on a bench as he sat alongside her. "I just need someone to watch my back, Khalid. I'm all alone out here, I don't have anyone," she said plaintively.

"Baby, you know I'm here to help you any way I can," Khalid reached over and brushed a lock of hair from her face.

"Don't get cute, scumbag," she slapped his hand from her face.

"You know, I don't think you need much help."

"It's like I told you this morning, I want to get inside, I want to go where the big boys meet. I think Adolf is gonna make a difference, I think he's gonna turn this community into a driving force. I wanna be a part of it, or at least get close enough to let him decide whether I can make a contribution. You've got to know where I'm coming from. It's bad enough to be living out here on the street, being outcasts from society. How can we turn down a chance to make a difference and still be free?"

"That's your problem, Roni," he stared at her. "There's too many angles to your story. It's hard to tell where you're coming from. You say you wanted to walk away, to live your life, to see the world, but here you are in New York City. Why aren't you riding the rail, out absorbing the country? You talk like a hobo, live like a bag lady, yet have plans to climb the volcano."

"What about you, Khalid?" she met his gaze. "You say you came from the Vaishya, your parents were wealthy entrepreneurs, yet you came here to be a lowly Shudra."

"Shudras work for a living," he said mockingly.

"Don't be an ass," she snapped.

"You know, you sure strapped your tits on quick enough. Are you a cop?"

"What?"

"Just thought I'd ask. Look, I'll be your road dog, I'll watch your back, and we'll get inside together. Getting in with the hoboes is a lot different than sleeping under a bridge or in a train station. They live in their own world, and it can get dangerous. Sometimes people go in and they disappear, no one ever hears from them again. If you want in, I'll go with you, but I'm giving you fair warning."

"Just like that?" she was skeptical.

"There's something I like about you," he smiled softly. "I think I'll like hanging out with you."

"All right," she stood up. "I already got my own spot, so you're gonna have to find a bush of your own."

Khalid tagged along, and soon they were at the treeline near the reservoir. They found soft spots under the bushes where they soon fell asleep, comfortable in knowing they had someone else watching their backs.

Chapter Six

When construction workers arrived at their worksite near 30th Street and 10th Avenue at daybreak, they found a crowd of homeless people congregated at the entrance to the crosslink fenced area. As the foremen inquired, the vagrants insisted they were there to attend a rally and would not disperse. The police arrived and the crowd disbanded, only they split into groups and continued to loiter at the nearest street corner. Once news began traveling, greater numbers of homeless people began arriving at the worksite where they were redirected by beleaguered police. As they reconvened at nearby intersections, more and more police were summoned to direct them elsewhere.

Veronika Heydrich marveled at the genius of Adolf Hyatt's strategy as the event progressed. This would probably be all over the airwaves once word got out, and undoubtedly the Mayor would be issuing a public statement. The unwashed masses continued to surge upon the area, and though they were ordered to leave the vicinity, they merely walked to the nearest corner and remained until they were confronted by the NYPD anew. It was straining the police's resources to the max, and most of the vagrants were unaware of the effect their very presence was having on the overall situation.

Hyatt appeared with his Disciples about fifteen minutes after the police arrived. They were distributing flyers consonant with his speech the previous day, and Hyatt argued his freedom of assembly with officers who demanded that he vacate the area. Hyatt merely took his act down the street as did his fellow vagrants, where yet another group of police officers awaited. They eventually ran into mobile broadcast units from local TV stations, eager for a live on-the-scene interview with Hyatt. He launched into a tirade about the vagrants' Constitutional rights being violated before going on into how they were being dispossessed by the obliteration of the railroad yards. It opened up a whole new dialogue on the Hobo Underground, spotlighting Hyatt as the King of the Hoboes.

"Okay, here's our chance," Veronika insisted. "Let's get in close with one of his main men and see if we can help move the flyers or do something useful."

"Yeah, like keeping from getting our heads cracked open," Khalid grunted.

They nudged and wheedled their way through the crowd surrounding the Hyatts, and eventually Veronika got up close enough to a towering, bearded Disciple who stood glowering at those who came too close to Hyatt and his entourage.

"Hey, we wanna help," Veronika insisted. "Let us hand out some flyers."

"Sure, why not," he shrugged. Although the Hyatts were enjoying a superior show of numbers, few were stepping up to support them in the face of the police. He beckoned to one of the Followers, who split his stack of flyers and handed half over to Veronika. She, in turn, handed half of them over to Khalid. They remained within view of the Disciple as they handed out flyers to passersby, shilling for Hyatt in telling them what a great man he was.

Hyatt stood his ground about two blocks away from the construction site, with police officials urging restraint from their units and the press having a field day with the spontaneous combustion of the event. Veronika was impressed by the fact that he changed character entirely, switching over from his Resolver martyr complex to a social reformer. He responded to every argument with a compelling recital of legal and historical precedent, silencing even the grizzliest reporters with his rhetoric. After it seemed that all they had left was kitchen-and-garden 'In your opinion' questions, Hyatt turned majestically and walked away from the spectacle. The horde of vagrants followed in his wake as he walked along the Yards to where the fencelines finally ended. There he had arranged for community service vehicles to meet them, and the vagabonds were treated to free coffee and soda as Hyatt walked out towards a clearing overlooking the Hudson River.

"Hey, Ad, these two've been tagging along since the party started," the bearded giant called over to Hyatt as he took a seat on a dirt-caked park bench. "They say they wanna get involved. I was trying to set up a time to meet with them tomorrow but the lady can't wait."

"It's not just me, it's the hundreds of other women and children on the street who have no one to speak for them," Veronika walked over to where Hyatt sat with legs crossed and arms draped over the bench like a casual stroller at rest. "I nearly got jumped by five gangbangers last night if Khalid hadn't come by and got me out of it. It's just like you said at the lot yesterday morning, this city's kicking the homeless women and children out to the curb. I want to help you reach out to the people who can do something in any way I can."

"Seems like you came at an opportune time," Hyatt grinned. "As you can see, we don't have any women in our inner circle at present. I think we should have at least one female voice so that women are fairly represented among us. As for your little friend, one of my close associates has had to leave town on personal business. I think he may be a suitable replacement for now. What's your names?"

"I'm Roni, and that's Khalid."

"Well, at the risk of being called Jesus, you are now being included among my Disciples, and I'm gonna call you my Mary Magdalene and him my Judas."

"Hey, I'm no traitor," Khalid objected, "and I definitely am not a rat. My name's solid on the street, you check around."

"Judas is what Judas does, and that goes for each and every one of us. I am no Resolver if I bring no resolution, and you are no traitor if you do not betray."

"Sounds fine by me. I'd prefer Khalid, if you don't mind."

"Go get you and Roni something over at the truck. I'm sure you're both thirsty."

Roni found herself a place to sit by one of the trees left standing in the area, and she had a chance to watch Hyatt work his magic. Vagrants came to him at regular intervals to stop and chat, sometimes to have extended conversations. All the while, Hyatt's black-clad Disciples patrolled the area, occasionally stopping to sit on the grass well within earshot of where Hyatt was. They kept close watch over him, and there was not a time when at least one of them knew exactly who was talking with him about what.

At length, a couple of the go-fers came along with two large cardboard boxes. They gave them to the Disciples, who set them in front of the bench before Hyatt. He reached in and picked out a loaf of Italian bread and a can of potted meat before beckoning the Disciples to come and get some. Both Veronika and Khalid were surprised and grateful to be called over, and they graciously picked out bread and canned meat before retreating back to their spot by the tree. They both had a spare can of soda, and they contentedly made sandwiches while

Hyatt asked his men to carry the boxes onto the field so other vagrants could help themselves.

Most of this seemed just too good to be true, and she considered the other Christ-like figures in history who turned out to be demonic when the opportunity arose. She recalled that Charles Manson and Jim Jones were but two of the cult figures who brainwashed their followers to ridiculous lengths. She knew that Hyatt was coaching the homeless into monumental acts of civil disobedience, but so far no one had gotten hurt though large areas of the City did stink of piss a couple of weeks ago. She could not figure what they would possibly be able to bust him for, and she might find herself having to frame Hyatt to earn her detective's badge.

"We have a private shelter in Brooklyn Heights," one of the Disciples came over after Veronika and Khalid had eaten. "We'd like you both to come join us."

"Uh—sure," she managed, her eyes widening momentarily when she considered they would have to walk the length of Manhattan and cross the Brooklyn Bridge to get to where she was sure they were going. These were walking mofos, but she had gone way too far to back down now.

Veronika was impressed by the fact that they walked in separate groups of three, which made them seem unconnected though having a large section of concrete covered between them. The one who walked with her and Khalid was called Bartholomew, a bearded man standing 6'4" and weighing 300 pounds. Though they had to hustle to keep up with him and the other fast-walking Disciples, both she and Khalid felt more at ease than they had in a long while.

It took them two hours to walk down Broadway and cross the side streets en route to the Brooklyn Bridge. It had been years since she had crossed on the pedestrian walk, and if her feet had not hurt so bad it would have been an enjoyable sojourn. She had watched in fascination as the Disciples had managed to panhandle while the group made its way down the thoroughfare without losing a step. They would then break off from the main group and make purchases at delis as they passed by, buying what they needed and trotting to catch up with Hyatt afterwards with their groceries. Hyatt would have a couple of bites of a sandwich or a piece of fruit, a sip from a bottle, then it would be passed along. All the time the great procession continued, the flying column making its way down the street sustaining itself without once breaking stride.

As she watched, she realized how they made it all seem so simple. Each of the Disciples was a handsome man in his own way, charming and personable, the kind of man you would engage in conversation on the street or join in assisting one in need. They were the kind of men you would see moving in next door and be glad that this was the new neighbor. Only the clothes they wore might raise a question as to their character, and even then one might consider that they were down on their luck and would surely rise again.

When they reached the Bridge, the formations changed as now the group in front had joined into a five-man band, leading the way along the boardwalk about twenty yards ahead of Hyatt and three disciples, who were then followed at an equal distance by Veronika, Khalid, Bartholomew and two other disciples, James II and Simon II. They were both big, strapping men, as personable and outgoing as Bartholomew. He had been regaling Veronika and Khalid with tales of the road, anecdotes about the hobo life. When James and Simon joined in, it made it sound as if it was like joining the circus, the most wonderful and adventurous thing anyone could ever devote themselves to.

She saw the purpose of them shifting to the five-four-five group formation, especially when a quartet of gangbangers, a young couple, and a cop on the beat walked by at intervals. The group of five was gregarious, carefree, resembling a bunch of students on a day off. Plus the size of the men would discourage anyone from either running afoul of them, or doing anything that would cause them to intervene. In the middle of all of it was Hyatt, the shepherd listening, nodding, giving advice or encouragement to his flock. They all ministered to his every need, and he to theirs with his words and looks of approval.

At long last the crossed the Bridge, and they made their way down to the rows of industrial buildings and warehouses along the dimly-lit streets. It was well known that a few of the buildings were owned by the Watchtower Society, the great digital clock on their World Headquarters overlooking the East River for the better part of a century. Most were used for storing surplus and outdated printing machinery and supplies from their enormous publishing industry, and some had been set aside as shelters for the homeless. Hyatt and his Disciples had converted one into their own stronghold, and Veronika and Khalid had become one of the chosen few who were permitted to step inside.

"You must remember the old legend of the fishermen who sailed into the eye of the storm," Jude led Veronika and Khalid into a large bay area within the warehouse. Fourteen cots had been set out with a pillow and blanket on each of them. "They had sailed that lake all their lives, they knew the storm was coming, yet they set sail anyway. They knew their boat could be overturned, and they could all lose their lives. They also knew they weren't going to catch any fish on this trip. Their only purpose was to see if the Master could rescue them. And he did. He walked from the shore across the water, through the storm to them. He calmed the storm, got in the boat and joined them. Together they sailed to the other side of the lake. There was never a question of him saving them, or whether he could calm the storm. They just wanted to share the experience."

"So you gonna stay here with these guys?" Khalid asked as they picked a couple of cots in the far corner of the darkened room. There was a large candle-lit room off to the far left at the other end of the hall, and a smaller room right next to it that seemed to be Hyatt's sanctum sanctorum. The Disciples were going in and out, exchanging words with Hyatt as they went to and fro. "You know, I can make us enough to get by out there. These guys are gonna want something sooner or later. They're gonna want us to hustle for them. I can hustle enough for both of us, we don't have to cut them in."

"Yeah, and what?" Veronika grunted. "You do some married lady, and her husband comes looking for you and cuts you open? Or suppose you get AIDS or herpes, or gonorrhea or some damn thing? Get over it, kid, there's better ways to make a living."

"Yeah, like what, getting a job and going to work?" he sneered.

It was here where she had to watch her step lest she stumble and give the scam away. It was in her nature to be of good counsel to the point of being pedantic. If it were not for her adventurous spirit and her need for speed, she would have made a good psychologist or social worker. She fought desperately with her desire to preach to the lost sheep among the computer hackers and the drug dealers. There was always the poor soul who had lost their way and wandered off amidst the pack of wolves. She also knew that sometimes these types were planted in the group as a decoy to draw out the betrayers, and she had heard of a number of undercover cops who lost their lives reaching out to them. Veronika would never be so foolish, though the tendency always lingered.

"I'm gonna use the restroom and wash up," she announced as she headed for the lavatory in the opposite corner off to their left. She walked across the thirty-foot room and opened the door, and was astonished at a trucker gas station-quality restroom complete with a shower in the rear area. She knew that this had been something installed by the Jehovah's Witnesses, and she decided to take full advantage.

Here she figured on playing the gambit, heading over to the shower area and stepping into the last stall. She figured that if they raped her, Evan was out there somewhere, and if she fled screaming into the night they would have their arrest, as poorly as it was concocted. Raping an undercover cop was not going to get it, and whoever's DNA showed up in the tests was going away for a considerable length of time. At the least, she would find out how trustworthy Khalid was, whether he really had her back (and her ass).

Veronika was exhilarated by the warm water as the strong spray buffeted her skin, and she scrubbed her hair as best she could with the tiny bar of motel-class soap available. Her hair was so long and thick that she might well have considered cutting it for this job. She always put up with jokes about her golden fleece, but no one could ever deny how beautiful it was. She had twice as much trouble as the next girl in grooming herself, but knew she would not be able to afford herself any luxuries on this case.

She decided to soak her hair and let it dry itself, even though it was going to be frizzy as hell tomorrow, especially without the benefit of a brush. She had picked up a comb in her travels but it was going to be as much use as a broom on a thick rug in the morning. When she finally cut the water off, she used her hoodie to towel herself before dressing. She would soak her panties and socks again and drape them over her boots to dry overnight.

The toilet flushed a couple of times and the door opened and closed, but no one even called over or commented about her being back there. She finally emerged from the lavatory, noticing that six of the Disciples had taken cots by the doors and were in various stages of repose. She made her way over to where Khalid was, lying down on the corner cot beside his.

"They said they passed your test, and they hoped you would pass theirs," Khalid said drowsily. Veronika laid down on the cot beside him, and at once her body was thrilled with the feel of the canvas as it cradled her. She had been sleeping on the ground since Monday, and this was as a stage of nirvana. She closed her eyes and stretched, and within minutes she was sound asleep.

Evan Carlow had tracked Hyatt, his Disciples, Veronika and the Indian teen to the warehouse and found himself in an alleyway just down the street. He had been going on REM sleep since this assignment began on Monday, and it was the severest test he had undergone since he was an eighteen-year-old serving in Iraq. He was doing his best to keep tabs on Veronika, and in doing so barely had a chance to eat or sleep. He was carrying a cell phone and his Glock, and had arranged to have sandwiches and drinks dropped off by patrol cars a couple of times. They would drive up to a trash can and toss the paper bag in, and he would pick it up once they drove off and no one was looking. He felt terribly guilty, knowing that Veronika was barely making it out there. Yet he knew that her safety depended on him being able to respond as quickly as possible if anything went sideways.

He heard movement behind him before he saw anything, and when he whirled around the two men were almost upon him. They were a couple of big burly bastards, and they tried to tackle him but he managed to launch a front kick that caught the closest man in the groin. He staggered into Evan as the second man flew into both of them, knocking them to the ground. Evan rolled backwards as the man pulled a bayonet with a foot-long blade from its sheath. He dropped back in a defensive stance as the man came forth, blocking with his left, the blade turned upwards to slice into any blocking motion.

The man pounced forth, and Evan had no choice but to throw out his forearm to keep the blade from stabbing him in the gut. It ripped an inch-deep slice into his arm, and he threw a desperate right cross which smashed the man across the jaw. Evan rolled backwards, whipping his Glock loose from his ankle holster as he had practiced hundreds of times over the years. The two men straightened up as the first one dropped the bayonet, knowing he had the drop on them.

"Okay, you sons of bitches, back towards Cadman Plaza. If you make a stupid move I'll put one in your feckin' heads."

The men marched steadily, evenly, as captured military men were wont to do. Blood was running from Evan's forearm, dripping onto his clothing and leaving a slight trail behind him. The man with the blade knew the best place to cut. They walked up the incline from the cobblestoned streets underneath the Bridge, and the hike seemed unusually steep as he was steadily losing blood. He knew after they stitched it his left arm would be next to useless tomorrow. Even worse, he was going to have to figure out how the hell he would pick up Roni's trail.

By the time they reached Cadman Plaza East, he was feeling as if he had guzzled down a six pack. The two assailants turned to look at him, and he ordered them down on their knees with their hands behind their heads. He then pushed them with his boot so that they fell forward face first on the grass bordering the sidewalk. A car slowed down to rubberneck as he kept his gun trained on the men.

"I'm a cop!" he yelled at the driver. "Call the police!"

By the time the police arrived, Evan put his gun on the ground as they approached with pistols drawn. He started to identify himself but slowly sank into unconsciousness.

Chapter Seven

Evan Carlow was taken to Long Island College Hospital on Hicks Street, where he was given a transfusion after losing nearly two pints of blood. The blade had cut his radial artery and required emergency surgery. Just as he suspected, they put his arm in a sling and Sgt. Andrade was there to put him on medical leave.

"No way," Evan insisted as Andrade paid him a bedside visit. Andrade was a tall, slender desk jockey with a balding pate and a well-trimmed red beard. "There's no way in hell I'm leaving my partner out there with no backup. I'm going right back out, you tell Lieutenant Shreve that. There's no way in hell they made me. I was dressed in black, wearing a ball cap, and we were in an alley with no lighting. I ditch this brace and I'm just like a thousand other guys out there."

"Don't you think you may be placing Officer Heydrich in greater danger if her backup's only got one wing?" Andrade peered over his wire-rimmed glasses.

It was Thursday morning, and the two assailants were booked and taken to Manhattan Central Booking. Fingerprints would eventually reveal Bob Jackson, an Army Ranger who had served in Operation Desert Storm in '91, and Bill Hunter, a Marine Recon veteran who served in Afghanistan. It explained to Evan how the two men came up on him so silently, and further indicated the quality of men Hyatt recruited into his inner circle. They were being charged with attempted manslaughter of a police officer. The charges would not hold up in court, but they were serious enough to keep both men off the street and put them in solitary confinement so Hyatt could not communicate with them.

"I still got my cell phone, I can call backup if it comes to that," Evan replied as he rolled out of bed, going to the closet for his clothes. "I don't know how those two goons made me. They must've had people staked out on watch outside that warehouse. I think I'm starting to see something. Hyatt's got a sophisticated support network. Guys like Jackson and Hunter didn't leave the service to sign up with some raggedy-ass crew of stink bums. Somehow he's earning the allegiance of these types of men. I've served alongside these kinds of guys. They don't like taking orders, but when they accept an authority they'll enforce it to the death. I saw Veronika in the middle of twelve of those guys, and I'm damn sure not leaving her alone out there with them."

"You know Bob Methot just came off administrative leave, and he's raring to go," Andrade suggested. "We could put him in for a couple of days, that'd give you time to rest that arm. I can't think of anyone she'd be safer with than Methot."

"I can," Evan fell back and pulled on his dungarees with one hand. "Me."

Veronika woke up that morning and was delighted to see a couple of hoboes bringing in a sack of Egg McMuffins and cardboard trays full of coffee cups. Khalid pounced out of bed and the Disciples moved aside so he could get some for himself and Veronika.

"Addy hoped you and the boy had a good night's rest," Thaddeus spoke from alongside her, and she was startled to realize she never knew he came up on her.

"Beats the heck out of sleeping on the grass," she agreed as Khalid came back with their breakfast.

"We're gonna do a soapbox on Wall Street around lunchtime," Thaddeus told them. "You two down?"

"Sure, we're all in," Veronika turned to Khalid. "Right?"

"Uh, yeah," Khalid agreed. "All in."

Simon Peter came out from Hyatt's office and told them all they would meet at 14 Wall Street at the corner of Broad and Wall. The Disciples filed out of the warehouse, and Veronika and Khalid followed them out to find they split into pairs. They took off in their usual double-speed, long-legged pace, and soon disappeared around the street corners out of sight.

"Let's try and catch up, see where they go," Veronika nudged Khalid, then broke out in a trot to the northwest corner of the street. He caught up with her and they watched as one of the pairs of Disciples turned a corner going up towards Memorial Park at Cadman Plaza. Khalid followed Veronika as they sprinted along, and they eventually caught sight of Thomas and Simon II at

Memorial Park. The two men were met by four others, each of who handed envelopes to the Disciples before going their separate ways.

"That almost looks like a drug payoff," she marveled. "Let's tail the guy headed down towards Flatbush Avenue and see where he goes."

"I don't think we should mess with these guys," Khalid was dubious. "I've seen things. These people are not to be trifled with. I think you should consider getting me some work at the beauty salon. I'll go fifty-fifty with you, I swear."

"And what, I'm gonna be a lady pimp? Did you fall down and crack your skull? Look, I'm not trying to cut into anyone's action. I just want to make sure we're not getting in over our heads. Let's just get an idea of where the money's coming from, and we can make a decision from there."

"I've already made a decision. You are stupid. I am offering to cut you in for fifty percent for doing nothing. You are trying to bring me into a group of ruthless men to no profit whatsoever."

"Did you just call me stupid?" she squinted at him.

"There is an old saying in India," he said sagely. "If the shoe fits…"

"Come on, squirt," she grabbed his sleeve and dragged him along.

They watched at length as the bearded man walked to the intersection of Flatbush and Fulton, where he met a young black girl who was dressed very much like a hooker with out-of-style yet revealing 70's style clothing, including a tube top, hot pants and go-go boots. They spoke at length before she handed him a small envelope. They then continued their conversation before he looked around to see if they were being watched. Veronika grabbed Khalid and pulled him around as if horseplaying as they stood on a corner diagonally across from the hustlers. The man then had some parting words for the hooker before continuing down Fulton Street.

"I think I've seen enough," Veronika said as Khalid straightened out his jacket. He did not like Veronika being a head taller and a bit stronger than him, but there was not much he could do about it. "We'd better get a move on to the Bridge so we can make that rally."

"I resent you manhandling me like this," he dusted his sleeve where she had grabbed him. "I am the man, you know."

"Yeah, sure," she slapped him on the shoulder. "That's what all the guys tell me. Let's get a move on."

As they walked up the steps to the Bridge, they saw a number of homeless people heading across towards the Manhattan side. She was aware that it was getting harder and harder to identify vagrants by their attire alone, as quality hangout clothes was readily affordable in thrift stores. Plus the fact that young people were dressing more like recently released convicts, wearing droopy drawers without belts and wife-beater t-shirts, made it harder to discern who was who out here. Combined with that was the fact that almost everyone was carrying some sort of baggage these days (emotional or otherwise), from backpacks to fanny packs. You could barely tell street-smart teens from underprivileged street kids or homeless youths. Being in the middle of the Great Recession was hardly making it any easier for social workers, or cops, for that matter.

By the time they hit the Manhattan side, they found a large bunch of students from nearby campuses mingling with the homeless crowds. The students of the day were keenly aware of social problems, perhaps as much from their own families' dysfunctions as their realization of the discrepancies between their own standard of living and those of the next person. She tried not to be too cynical in considering how much their benevolent spirits would change once they were out in the real world fending for theirselves. It was a lot harder giving the shirt off one's back or the last dollar in one's pocket when there was no rich Daddy at home glad to replace it.

Veronika and Khalid followed the crowd as it surged towards Wall Street. She got a big kick out of the faces of the yuppie bankers and accountants staring in revulsion and apprehension at the unwashed masses invading their fiefdom. It also made her enjoy her masquerade all the more, thinking of how they would be leering at her with tongues hanging if she was down here in one of her dress suits. Yet she could not ignore the twinge of indignation in realizing what it would be like if she could not go back, if she were to remain one of the people they saw as human waste, if she could no longer afford to be who she was.

As they neared the Wall Street intersection, she was amazed at what Hyatt had achieved here. It was almost as a scene from *Les Miserables*, as the hordes of poor people rallied around the Resolver. He vented his rage against the monuments of greed that were the financial institutions towering above them, shaking his fist as the vagrants and the brokers alike stared in wonder. The police arrived and took up positions around the crowd, none of whom remotely considered a confrontation and a possible crack over the head.

"Look around you!" Hyatt had already started his harangue despite the fact it was well before noon. He had started off talking to a couple of students before a few rookie bankers came by and began questioning his motives. He eagerly engaged them in debate, with two of his massive Disciples standing on either side of him as he lambasted him from atop his milk crate. Once he got on a roll there was no stopping him, and enough students and vagrants had gathered so that he was able to begin preaching in earnest to the motley crowd.

"Look around you!" He gestured dramatically upwards at the majestic buildings appearing as the walls of a great canyon encompassing them. "Do you not think that if they sold just one, only one of these buildings and gave the money to the poor, each and every one of you would not have enough to buy clothes as nice as what the man next to you is wearing?"

"Heck, I think I would be worse off than I am right now," a vagrant standing between two hoboes cracked, evoking a round of laughter from his neighbors.

"Why don't you tell 'em to get a job?" a broker called out belligerently.

"Why don't you lend one of them that $300 dollar suit you're wearing and see whether or not they come back as your supervisor?" Hyatt demanded. "Do you believe the hype from your *Wall Street* movie, that the difference between you and them is your work ethic? Do you think you worked harder pushing your pencil in your ivory tower while half of these men were digging foxholes in foreign deserts, fighting for your right to push those pencils? Do you think you worked harder to keep your job while their companies collapsed along with the economy, and this Government of yours took away their homes, their cars, and everything they had? Do you think you were more industrious when you invented those Ponzi schemes that liquidated their savings accounts and their investment programs? Woe unto you swindlers and defrauders! You cry out to these police officers for not chasing down the robbers and burglars prowling the streets for money to feed themselves. Yet you steal a hundred times as much with one stroke of a pen!"

"You're up here running us down, yet we're the ones paying the taxes that put those welfare cards in your pockets!" an accountant yelled at him. "The Government's taking almost half my money. I'll bet they'll never see a penny of yours."

"Spoken like a true Republican!" Hyatt called back. "How much're you making there, brother? Half a million a year? Or maybe your boss is making that, and you're only making half of what he does. Tell you what, I'll be willing to split half of what you're making with the Government, I'd have no problem with that at all. Now, I know that there would be lots of privileges I would have to exchange in order to earn that kind of money. I would have to sit in an overstuffed chair seven and a half hours a day in front of a big glass window overlooking this entire area, in a temperature-controlled environment with some fine-looking, big-legged secretary at my beck and call. In order to do that, I would have to give up my freedom to walk the streets all day and beg for chump change just to buy a cup of coffee. That sounds like a mighty big trade, my friend. Let me ask our brothers and sisters here: how many of you would be willing to make that deal with these devils?"

A great roar rose from the crowd as many waved their hands in agreement. Those standing near the accountants heckled and ribbed them until they walked away in embarrassment.

"Hey, I got a good one for you all," Hyatt outstretched his arms. "Let's take a gander at that Federal Reserve Bank down the way there on Liberty Street. Now, that place is holding onto ten percent of the gold reserves on this entire planet. That's right, you can take a tour and check it out for yourselves. Now, just in case you get any wild ideas, I'll let you know up front that each of them bars weighs twenty-eight pounds. They aren't them little bitty bars James Bond was chucking at Oddjob in that *Goldfinger* movie. Those guards working the late shift down there wear steel-tipped boots in case they drop one while they're moving them around."

"Why don't you see if you can get us some free samples?" a hobo called out to a round of raucous laughter.

"Hey, I'm working on that brother," Hyatt replied. "Now, at last count, that bank had assets of $1.75 trillion dollars. First of all, that's Federal reserves, as in backup money, like the money you keep in your sock instead of your wallet. Second of all, that's like a thousand billion bucks. If they gave that to you in singles, you'd die of old age before you could count your change."

"Heck, I'd be willing to die trying!" another man evoked a smattering of cheers.

"Check this out," Hyatt challenged them. "The national student loan debt, at last count, was $986 billion dollars. That comes out to about twenty-six grand per student, according to the Internet. That's about what these bankers pay for their wives' cars. Now, imagine a kid out of college, working at Mc Donald's because the job he studied for is maxed out of spots. Can you imagine him trying to pay that kind of note before covering his room and board? Why don't they just use all that reserve money to pay back that debt? They sure as heck forced them kids to take out those loans, telling them they would spend the rest of their lives working at Mc Donald's if they didn't."

There was another ovation from the crowd as all the students in attendance heard Hyatt's battle cry on their behalf. Most had heard nothing but horror stories from friends who had graduated, and realized they were facing a similar fate upon entering the work force.

"You'd better get some schooling, Hyatt!" a broker challenged him. "Why do you think we have Federal reserves? Would you cash in your 401k to pay off your wife's car loan?"

"I sure as hell would if my wife didn't have enough money left over to put gas in that car!" Hyatt shot back to a resounding cry of approval. "I'd be able to start a new 401k just as sure as you could rebuild your Federal reserve!"

Eventually the crowd had grown so large that the Disciples had to join ranks in front of Hyatt to keep him from being knocked off his milk crate. He saw a police van pulling up to the curb and realized they might call this a disturbance. He whispered instructions to his men before turning the crate right side up and disappearing into the audience.

"Now isn't that man just full of surprises," Veronika shook her head. "Let's head out to the Bridge before it turns into a mob scene down there."

She and Khalid darted through the crowd as it slowly dispersed, then broke into a trot as they cut down to Water Street and hit the Bridge before most everyone else. They enjoyed the stroll across the boardwalk more than last night in not having to keep pace with the Disciples. They were both in a good mood though they did not discuss what Hyatt had said or the crowd's reaction. She did not want to compromise her cover by having Khalid think she was any more than a common street person, and would hardly want to get into any deep theoretical discussions.

It did not take rocket science for them to figure out how the Hyatts were already back at the warehouse by the time they arrived. She was pretty sure they had not jumped the turnstiles either, so apparently they came up with the twenty-two bucks' worth of tokens needed to make the short trip. It would not have been the message he wanted to convey to his followers, so perhaps there were just two in particular he wanted to impress.

A couple of Followers had shown up with their daily bread in the form of provisions from the local soup kitchen, and Peter brought the bag first to Hyatt, then Veronika and Khalid before the others. She surmised that there was a lot of

59

messaging going on here in giving the two newcomers first dibs. They seemed to be going out of their way in making them feel at home, and she was just waiting to see how the other boot would drop.

She felt as if it was a lot nicer being a bum in Brooklyn as opposed to one in Manhattan. There were a lot fewer people around Memorial Park, and the police were not as brusque as long as one kept moving and did not get spotted panhandling. Khalid suggested they move down by the River Café on Water Street where not only wealthy motorists cruised along, but there were plenty of directions to run if the cops got ornery.

She took turns sitting and standing on the concrete foundation to one of the support beams of the Bridge where a beggar had left a plastic bucket. Khalid would offer to wipe windshields in exchange for chump change, and dumped the proceeds into Veronika's bucket. They were doing well, and more than a number of male drivers offered to take her for a ride. She graciously declined, glad to see that she was still seen as attractive though most were probably looking for little more than a quickie.

"Hey, you! Scuzzball! Get over here!" a voice yelled, accompanied by the whoop of a patrol car. Veronika watched as Khalid rushed onto the curb, watching from a short distance, as a stray dog concerned for the well-being of the last person who fed him.

"Yes, sir," Veronika tried to act like she dreaded being taken to Central Booking.

"Glad we found you," the cop on the passenger side said in a muted voice through taut lips so Khalid was unable to eavesdrop. "Carlow's been going nuts looking for you. He got knifed the other night but he's back on the case. You hang around here for a little bit and we'll have him back on your tail."

"Oh my gosh," she managed. "Is he okay?"

"He's back on the street, sugar puss. You be careful, okay?"

"Roger that."

"Hey, shithead!" the cop whooped his siren again as he hit the brakes alongside Khalid. "Keep the hell outta the street! Go take a bath!"

"Buzz off, flatfoot," Khalid muttered.

"What'd you say?" the cop opened the car door. Khalid raced to the fence surrounding the downslope from the highway access road, hopping over before running out of sight. With that, the cop winked at Veronika before the patrol car made its way back into traffic.

She waited until the vehicle disappeared before climbing over the fence to look for Khalid. She had not far to go as he sat on the crest of the slope, ready to cut and run if the cops came around the entranceway in hopes of roughing him up.

"Good thing it's rush hour, or they would've caught me for the sport of it."

"They would've probably kicked your ass," she pointed out. "Let's go back down to Flatbush, those guys probably work the Heights."

The two of them walked back down to Flatbush where Khalid found a discarded Work for Food sign and stood on the corner for a couple of hours while Veronika found another bucket to guard at curbside. She was greatly distracted by what the cop had told her and hoped Evan was okay. She could not figure out what had provoked the attack, and judging from what she had seen on the street, it could have been a number of things. She looked around now and again, hoping to see his face in a crowd but knew that he was far too good at what he did to get spotted that easily.

It finally grew dark and they decided to call it a day. They were surprised to have split about twenty bucks apiece. They both decided to stash their cash and see whether the Hyatts would have anything to eat before spending any money. Veronika also decided that she would go to the dollar store the first thing in the morning and get herself some things to put in a travel bag. She would forego any cosmetics but would pick up a toothbrush, toothpaste, toilet paper, anti-perspirant and anything else that would relieve the feeling of being the Grunge Lady of Brooklyn Heights.

When they got back to the warehouse, they were mildly disappointed to find that the Disciples had brought in a few platters of deli-style *oeurves*, including rabbit food, crackers and cold cuts. On the upside, they had a few bottles of 1975 vintage Bartsac/Sauternes red wine which nearly caused Veronika to marvel, only to do so would have blown her cover. She once again realized that it might have been a shrewd move to force her hand, and she played it like a street lady who didn't know champagne from port.

Hyatt was in good spirits as he came out to pop corks and pour everyone a plastic stemmed glass in a toast to their good fortune. The Disciples were also in a jovial mood and encouraged Veronika and Khalid to help themselves to some snacks. She joined them in their toast, and gladly accepted another glass of the Chateau Suduiraut Sauternes with its nectarine aftertaste. She was feeling fine after her second glass and took a seat on one of the bean bags strewn around the floor, chilling out as the Disciples traded jokes and anecdotes.

At length she noticed three good-looking teenage girls making their way into the warehouse entrance. The girls seemed as surprised by the interior of the place as Veronika and Khalid were. They were greeted by the Disciples and offered refreshments, and were very happy to be given some of the excellent wine. They were ushered over by the dark candlelit room off to the left of Hyatt's office where Veronika had yet to inspect.

As Veronika saw them being given purple robes and sent off to the lavatory, she suddenly had a feeling of light-headedness. She had a strong feeling that someone had put something like Rohypnol in her drink, but had no way of knowing for sure. She had not eaten much today and it was entirely possible that the fine wine was packing an extra punch. She lay back on the bean bag, feeling very comfortable as the enhanced sedative effect began kicking in. Khalid also seemed as if he had landed in Palookaville, his eyes drooping as he set a full glass untouched beside his own bean bag.

She watched the entrance to the candlelit as the girls were led in one by one. A purple curtain had been drawn over the threshold so that the activity remained unseen from the outside. It seemed as if each of them were in there for an inordinate length of time, though she was so messed up that she couldn't tell a minute from an hour. They were seated at a pew by the entrance, and the two that awaited the first girl nodded off to sleep and had to be awakened to take their turns.

The first girl was nearly staggering by the time she was brought out, replaced by the second girl. Veronika was feeling some strange vibes coming from the room, almost a palpable sense of evil. She blew it off as a side effect of the mickey, but it lashed at her senses nonetheless. She nearly started to doze off herself when she felt yet another presence, and when she looked up it was Adolf Hyatt himself.

"Do you dare step into the pentagram?"

"I dare anything," she looked at him through drooping eyelids. "I already told you that."

The effects of Rohypnol are such that the victim suffers a temporary form of amnesia and is unable to recall events while under influence of the drug.

Veronika found herself unable to remember anything from the time Hyatt took her by the hand and led her to the room. Her next recollection was lying naked on the floor inside the candlelit room, with Hyatt standing over her.

"Okay, you passed the test," Hyatt leaned over her and patted her face. "You're gonna be my Mary Magdalene. We'll see you tomorrow morning at daybreak. Don't sleep too late."

Unfortunately she was unable to comply with Hyatt's request, knocking out until nine AM the next morning. She found herself in her cot, with Khalid still in a state of slumber though his eyelids were beginning to flutter. She was fully clothed but had the strange feeling that someone had yanked her clothes up over her.

At once her loins were wracked with pain, her puss feeling as if someone had penetrated it with a battering ram. Her butt was also sore and she knew that she was going to have a major problem sitting down. They had also squeezed her tits like a dairy cow, and she wouldn't be surprised if she could see fingerprints. They had pulled a train over her, and she was swept by a feeling of outrage though she had no clue as to who had done the deed or how they went about it.

"Oh, my gosh," Khalid moaned as he managed to look around. "Where am I?"

"How's your butt doing?"

"I—uh—oooh," he gasped painfully. "What in hell—!"

"We just got initiated by the Hyatt Clan," she managed to keep calm. "Let's get the hell out of here while those rapist bastards are away. We need to re-group."

"They did my butt?" Khalid was outraged. "Why, I'll—!"

"Chill out, kid," Veronika insisted, managing to get to her feet despite the stabbing pain. "Somebody needs to take these guys down, and now we got a good reason why. I'll bet you ten to one they jumped those girls who went in that room over there."

She made her way over to the candlelit room and was taken aback by the sight of a large pentagram painted on the black-tiled floor. The room was decorated by black candles and occult statues and ornaments, and it was obvious that the Hyatts were practicing Satanism in here. She and Khalid, and most likely the three girls, had been made part of the ceremony and were probably considered part of the inner circle.

It was a big break in the case, but she was paying too high a price for her gold badge and was determined the Hyatts were going to pay as well.

Chapter Eight

Veronika insisted that Khalid accompany her on the train ride back to Manhattan, and they took the short ride on the N Train on the BMT line to Prince Street. They got to her loft building around ten AM, and she located her hideout keys in one of the flowerpots in front of the place to let them in.

"Aha!" Khalid exclaimed. "I knew there was more to you than being a homeless person. You must be part of some reality TV show!"

"Not hardly," she said as she unlocked the front door to let them in. "This is a friend's place who lets me come by in case of an emergency. Well, this is an emergency."

They rode the elevator to the second floor, and she was glad none of the neighbors were home to see her arrive in such a slovenly manner. She opened the door and she was filled with relief at being back home for the first time that week.

"Okay, listen," she told him, "we can chill out here a while and take a time out. I'm going to grab some things and we're back out the door. We need to catch up to Hyatt and find out what he'll be up to next."

"I told you these were dangerous people!" he insisted. "Haven't you had your fill of them? What do you think they'll do to us next if we go back? Suppose they were trying to break us in so we can go out and sell our asses next? Or are you one of those masochist-type people?"

"Don't get smart," she retorted, stifling a yawn. She was still feeling exhausted and her whole body hurt. She was going to have to catch a nap before they continued. "Look, I need to crash for a little bit. Let's chill for about three hours, and then we can head back towards the Bridge and find out where Hyatt's gone."

"As you wish," he replied. "I'm going to check out a little TV."

She shuffled off to her bedroom and dropped face first on the bed, nearly blacking out before having the presence of mind to pull herself up to where she could lay her head on the pillows. Normally she would have beat herself up for crawling into bed with dirty clothes such as these. She was hardly about to chastise herself in such a state as this, and dropped dead as a doornail in descending into a dreamless sleep.

She had no idea how long she was out, and only the smell of sweat and grime in her clothes and hair brought her to her senses. She saw that the sun was beginning to ebb outside, and knew they had to get back on the street and back to the Hyatt lair before they were crossed off the welcome list. Only she found herself naked with Khalid lying beside her, and knew that she had been jumped outside of her knowledge for the second time in less than twenty-four hours.

"You little son of a bitch!" she clamped a cross-face chicken wing on him, causing him to wake up with a scream of pain caught in his throat. "Did you just screw me while I was out?"

"Why did you bring me up here? Did you not think I desired you? Why do you think I have stood by you all this time since I met you?" he asked angrily after rolling off the bed.

"So you stuck with me just so you could get in my pants," she rolled off on the other side, throwing her closet door open to find some clothes. "You nasty little shit!"

"I am very attracted to you, Roni," he said quietly. "I want you to be my girl."

"Dumb little son of a bitch," she growled, pulling a terrycloth robe out of the closet. At once she heard a key in the lock in the door and broke a cold sweat.

"Who is that, the owner?" Khalid wondered.

"You wish," she scrambled past him and out into the living room.

She stared apprehensively at the sight of Evan Carlow in her doorway. He looked the worse for wear, holding his injured arm at an angle, his face covered by a two-day growth of stubble. His eyes were red from lack of sleep and the strain of living on the street was evident by the drawn look on his face.

"I figured you might've come back here for a breather," he managed a smile. "I've been tailing you and that kid for the last couple of days. When you hopped on the train I lost you but I had a hunch you were headed here."

Just then Khalid walked out from the bedroom, clad only in a pair of Veronika's khaki cargo shorts. He stared disapprovingly at Evan before resigning himself to the situation.

"I'm going to take a shower," he said sullenly, heading for the bathroom and locking the door behind him.

"Wait," Evan held his fingers to his temples. "I don't believe this shit. You screwed him."

"Look, it didn't happen just like that," Veronika's mind scrambled to concoct a story. "They put something in my drink last night. I came in here and passed out."

"Yeah?" Evan reached for his holstered gun at the back of his belt. "Then I'm arresting the little bastard for rape."

"No, you can't!" she insisted, blocking his path. "He's my road dog. If you bring him in I'll be going back naked, with no one watching my back."

"I'm watching your back," he flushed with anger.

"Look, the kid saved me from getting gangbanged in the park a couple of nights ago, and he's been watching me ever since. I screwed up, I shouldn't have passed out in bed like that. It was a dumb thing to do. Cut him some slack, I'm making some headway and I really need him with me."

"What kind of headway?" he demanded.

"I think Hyatt's got an extended network operating throughout Flatbush," she explained. "I think he's got street people pimping and selling drugs for him. You know how I am with hunches, I'm usually on the money, and I can smell this one. I'm onto something, I just need some more time and I need this kid."

"I guess you heard that one of those sons of bitches tried to cut me open the other night," Evan revealed. "There were two of them, we got their prints on Centre Street and it turns out they were Iraqi vets. I was down there yesterday at that Wall Street and saw all those big bastards he's got backing him up. You're in a hard situation in there, Roni. If they make you, there's no way I could get inside to pull you out. You think we can put a wire on you?"

"They just threw me buck-assed naked on top of a pentagram," she scowled. "I don't think that'd be a great idea."

"Well that's it, then," Evan said flatly. "You're coming out."

"Not on your life!" she thundered. "I've been living like a bum for almost a whole week and I got tossed in Central Booking, not to mention getting gangbanged. I'm getting that damn promotion, and if you don't like it *you* can come out!"

"What did you say?" he stared at her. "I thought you said the kid saved you from a gangbang."

"Not last night," she looked away, her voice growing husky. It really hadn't impacted her yet, and for some reason she was thinking more about the teenage girls. She couldn't help but think about how innocent and defenseless they seemed sitting outside the ritual room awaiting their turn.

"Roni, this is too much," he was adamant. "What did they do to you?"

"It was Rohypnol or some shit, I can't remember. You're a damn cop, you know how that crap works."

"You're both cops," suddenly Khalid reappeared in the doorway, still wearing her shorts. He had turned on the shower but had not stepped in yet. He appeared almost as if a child coming into the room in the middle of a fight between his parents, feeling dazed and confused. "And this is your apartment."

"That guy Hyatt is bad news," Veronika's heart went out to him despite the fact he had just screwed her while she was asleep. "The police are investigating him, they think he's planning something big. That deal we saw go down on Flatbush Avenue is just the tip of the iceberg. I need to go back in there and I need your help."

"I've seen too much," Khalid looked as if he was about to cry. "I know too much. If they knew what I know they'd probably kill me. I only went in there because of you. You've got him, you don't need me."

"She does need you, kid," Evan insisted. "I can only tail her from a distance. I can't go inside with her like you can. I can't protect her once she's in."

"Khalid," she informed him. "His name's Khalid."

"I'll tell you what I know," Khalid relented. "But then I'm out of here. I'll take a shower somewhere else."

Khalid then told them about the night beneath the bridge when the hoboes of the Four Corners were murdered by the campfire as they tried to sanction Hyatt. Khalid's stomach was sick with trepidation as he knew deep down that this couple would try and make him testify to the event if push came to shove.

"Dammit," Evan hissed once Khalid had finished his story. "You probably weren't close enough to make a positive identification. Twelve men with beards wouldn't hold up in court, and even if we made an arrest, we don't know who in hell it was that got murdered. Look, kid—Khalid—you just can't walk away from that. Someone loved those men, they were someone's sons, maybe someone's brothers or fathers. The Hyatts have to answer for what they did."

"Yeah, well, I'm somebody's son too, and what do you think you'll do about it if Roni and I get stabbed by twelve men with beards?"

"He's got a point," Veronika plopped down on a comfortable leather armchair.

"Stay out of this," he muttered before turning back to Khalid. "Look, those guys just raped your friend here. Can't you do this to help her out? Don't you think she deserves some kind of payback? Are you gonna let them get away with this?"

"They did you up too, don't forget," Veronika found a blessed cigarette and lit up, exhaling with great pleasure. She wasn't much of a smoker, enjoying one at times with a cordial. This was one of those occasions.

"What?" Evan jerked his head towards her.

"Well, it wasn't like I was a virgin, but I didn't get much pleasure out of it," Khalid admitted.

"So twelve guys dicked you up your arse, and you're gonna let them get away with it," Evan recovered.

"I'd rather take a dick than a bayonet," Khalid retorted.

"Look at it from their point of view," Veronica reasoned. "If we go back now, they'll figure we're solid. We went through their initiation and came back for more. You already saw how they went out of their way to make us feel comfortable before this. Now we passed their test, we'll be good as gold in there."

"What's in it for me?"

"A clear conscience, kid," Evan was emphatic. "Right now you're young and dumb and full of cum, and I mean that figuratively. But those murders won't go away, neither will the gang rapes. As you get older, those rapes and murders will keep coming back to haunt you, no matter how much alcohol you drink and how many drugs you take. You live on the street, you see those guys coming back from the war with those blank faces. The reason they look like that is because they have nightmares that don't go away when they wake up in the morning. They don't go away because they can't do anything to change what they saw over there. You can change the outcome. Maybe you can't change what happened, but you can make it right."

"Okay," Khalid exhaled. "I don't care about what they did to me, I can accept it. Those bums, though, they didn't need to get killed. They were just sitting around the campfire talking, and all of a sudden they got killed. No matter what was said, nobody deserves to die for just talking. I'll go back with Roni, but I can't promise you I'll stay in there. I'm not gonna risk my life around a bunch of dogs who kill people for just talking."

"Okay, kid," Evan walked over to where Veronika rose to face him. "I'm off. I'll be watching." He then hugged her and gave her a kiss before heading for the door.

"You make a good couple," Khalid admitted. "I won't stand between you."

"Gee, thanks, kid," Evan gave his best Harrison Ford imitation before taking off.

"All right, let's get some shower time and we're out of here," Veronika headed back towards her room.

"Care to join me?" Khalid grinned. She took off her sandal and threw it at him before he scampered back to the bathroom.

She looked around, then decided to pack the least expensive of her carryall bags with the barest necessities before going back out. She had already learned one of the biggest lessons of her life over the past few days and did not plan to make the same mistake twice.

She definitely would not make any false moves when confronting the Hyatts again.

Adolf Hyatt and four of his Disciples walked down to the River Café beneath the Brooklyn Bridge right about the time Evan Carlow had resumed his surveillance position not far from Veronika's apartment. They waited until the stretch limousine pulled up at the far side of the dock outside the Café, and Hyatt walked over to where a chauffeur held a passenger door open for him.

"Good afternoon, my friend," the bearded Arab wearing a *khalat* and designer suit welcomed him as they sat across from one another in the red-upholstered limo. "It is good to see you."

"I hope your people have made the arrangements," Hyatt stretched back, making himself comfortable as was his custom anywhere he went. "My people are ready to go."

"So these counterfeiters of yours have all these bills ready to dump out onto the streets of New York," the Arab stroked his beard.

"Not exactly. We're setting them out in five separate locations around Manhattan. We're not giving them out and we're not exchanging them for anything, we're merely putting the boxes out on the curb. What people do after that is beyond our control and not our concern. Of course, we're not keeping any secrets from the homeless community. Our brothers and sisters will all be privy to this unprecedented event in the history of social protest."

"This is well and good," the Arab bent forward. "Here is our proposition. We also plan to make a statement during that auspicious event. We will pay you ten million dollars to allow us to rendezvous at one of your strategic points on that day. We intend to strike a blow for Allah with the same impact, if not greater, than that which you lash out against the social injustices you suffer at the hands of the Great Satan."

"Well, I'll tell you, I'm not exactly at war with Satan," Hyatt chuckled. "I might even go as far as to say we're in cahoots. But I'm not gonna take his side in any squabble you and yours may have against him. Now, I think we discussed a Swiss bank account which you'll open for me and make a direct deposit on my behalf. What I'll need is a cell phone that I can use to confirm my account information. If, on the Day of Defiance, I see my money and everything's a go, then me and my boys walk away, and you and your boys drive up and do whatever you like next to that horde of scroungers grabbing that free money. On the other hand, if I don't see my money, I'll make sure the cops are right there as soon as me and my guys walk off."

"We have a deal, my friend," the Muslim shook Hyatt's hand.

Adolf Hyatt knew he had made yet another deal with the devil. It was just one of many he would continue to make as King of the Hoboes and self-proclaimed Scourge of New York City.

Chapter Nine

Veronika and Khalid arrived at the warehouse after dark, and she could tell by the looks on a couple of the Disciples' faces that they weren't fully expected to return. They were warmly greeted and directed to a couple of fruit baskets on a picnic table outside Hyatt's office door. It was as if nothing had happened, and she wondered which of them had gotten a piece of her while she was lying in the pentagram.

"Why, Mary and Jude have returned," Hyatt came out with a big grin, wearing a cheap Hawaiian shirt and khaki pants. "We hoped that after going off to reconsider, you would return to our crusade with greater determination than before."

"Like I told you, we're all in," Veronika said grimly. She did not want to give any of them the impression she was back for another gangbang. She wanted to express her feeling of betrayal over what they had done though not backing away from the Great Cause to which she had committed herself.

"Come on in," Hyatt made a sweeping gesture. They walked into the small room and were surprised to see that it was little more than a storeroom. There was a beat-up desk, a spindly swivel chair, a makeshift bookshelf made of cinder blocks and planks, and a couple of scratched-up folding chairs alongside it. "Please, have a seat. Now that you're part of our inner circle, I want you to be part of our plan to change the lives of the homeless community throughout New York City and across America."

Khalid appeared as taciturn as Veronika as they eyed Hyatt skeptically. She coached him to appear somewhat indignant, as the Hyatts did not know that Khalid was a male prostitute. She made him see the logic of booty duty being a greater indignity to a boy than a girl. She could not help but feel sad how Khalid had been abused all his life, and took such a thing as a matter of course. In a different time and place, she would have walked in here with a hand grenade. She was still eagerly awaiting the day when these bastards got sent away for a long, long time for whatever she could pin on them.

"As I'm sure you both can see, what we have done—what we are doing—is spreading concern and uncertainty throughout the community and the civic administration of this city. We have let them see what their neglect and abandonment of our people is costing them. Now, as far as I can see, despite all the publicity we've generated, our people have not seen one improvement or betterment of our situation. I feel it is time for us to take more aggressive action in drawing attention to our cause."

"Like what, putting a bomb under the Mayor's toilet seat?" Veronika was sarcastic.

"How about one on a few corners in some of the heavy traffic areas around town?" Hyatt smiled back.

"Whoa, wait, how's that?" Veronika stared at him.

"Paper bombs. The kind of bomb that will produce enough shrapnel to make the Boston Massacre look like a food fight."

"Hold on, boss man. I didn't sign up for anything like that."

"Not literal bombs or shrapnel, child. I'm talking about boxes full of funny money. Just think what would happen if all those high-rolling yuppies knew they could get their hands on some funny money they could easily pass off at the corner store. Why, I bet most of them would be elbowing our people out of the way to get to it. Even worse, I'd bet they'd be running to the nearest store so they could pass it off. Now, once those store owners got wind of what was happening, I bet they'd close up shop quicker than a *falafel* dealer in downtown Beirut during a bomb scare."

"So our next move is to disrupt the economy around town," Veronika frowned. "Don't you think the city economy's in enough of a mess?"

"Sometimes you have to take a child to the woodshed to make him learn a lesson," Hyatt shrugged. "We've tried numerous tactics to make these people think. It doesn't seem like we're getting through. It appears that more drastic measures may be called for. Now, dear sister, do you think I should just set our plans aside so that our people can continue to suffer more days?"

"I don't think your Disciples sat down with you long enough to help you think this through," Veronika replied. "Have you thought about what happens when news of this gets out? Counterfeiting is a Federal offense. If you put out more than one box of fake money, the Secret Service would be all over Manhattan, and they wouldn't be down here sightseeing. They'd be picking our people up left and right, and squeezing them hard with threats of doing time in a Federal pen. Not to mention the number of mentally ill people we got roaming the streets. There's going to be a lot of people downtown just because they couldn't give the right answers."

"Our purpose is to overburden them so they can step back and figure out how to redistribute their wealth," Hyatt said patiently. "How much of that money that they're pouring into the Hudson Docks, for example, really needs to be there right now? How much money are they spending on our streets and highways that could have been avoided if they did a quality job the first time? I can go on and on, but there are websites you can access that will bore you to tears about how much money is wasted on a daily basis. Suppose they do fill the jails with people suspected of passing funny money, and let the violent offenders go free? Don't you think it will make them take yet another pause to consider?"

"You remember how these last couple of Days of Defiance went down," she continued. "Private donors may withhold services and public services could run out of funds. If we paralyze the economy for one day, how're they gonna make the money back up?"

"These are the risks we have to take," Hyatt steepled his fingers.

"Just one more thing," Veronika said as they rose to leave. "What happened in that room the other night can't happen again. Not to us."

"And why should it?" Hyatt furrowed his brow. "You have made a flesh sacrifice to the higher spiritual power, you bonded with the Disciples and became one with them. This rite of passage never needs to be repeated. Does one go back and get baptized every year to reaffirm their Catholicism? Do we return to grade school after a time to renew our diploma? No, you both consummated your relationship with the Disciples, and it is finished. There is nothing left to give, no greater sacrifice. We are as one, forever and ever."

"Good to hear," she managed a smile. It crossed her mind that, if this had been a cartoon, she would be standing here with a star hovering over her ass. "Any idea what day this'll take place?"

"You'll be notified well in advance," he assured them.

"Boy, you sure told him," Khalid chortled as they headed outside. "I guess being a cop explains why you're so smart."

"Anybody hears you and I'll break your jaw," she elbowed him angrily.

"What are we gonna do?" he asked as they made their way towards Cadman Plaza. "No one is going to believe he is going to come up with boxes full of counterfeit money."

"I'm pretty sure he's full of shit," she decided. "He might have a bunch on top of the stack, but most of the box'll be full of play money or blank paper. If he had that much quality counterfeit, he sure wouldn't be giving it out on street corners."

"Maybe he's just testing us again, seeing if we'll snitch him out."

"I doubt it. He's feeling too strong right now. You could see in his eyes how it was turning him on. If we can find a way to catch him red-handed before he puts those boxes out, we'll put his ass out of business."

"Are you gonna call the Secret Service?"

"Hell no," she scoffed. "First of all, we don't know whether he's even got the money or if it's on order. No one wants to sit on a spot that hot. Plus, I want to take him down for killing those bums you mentioned, plus ass-raping us. Let's just see if we can find out where he's got the money coming from before we start planning anything."

Evan was sitting on the grass behind a stand of bushes, watching as Veronika and Khalid left the warehouse, walked up the block and crossed the street on Flatbush Avenue. He got up slowly and started coming out of the bushes when he saw two big men coming towards him across the grass.

"Hey, dude, got a light?"

One of the greatest hindrances in working undercover is the ever-present hazard of compromising one's cover. Once a cover is blown, it is as a game penalty which causes one's automatic ejection from the field. His Smith and Wesson was as big and bad as Darth Vader's light saber or Captain Kirk's phaser on his ankle, but once he drew it, if these guys pulled him off-side then he would have to resign his position for the remainder of the assignment.

That was not going to happen.

"No, I don't smoke."

"Oh, sorry about that, man," one of the men said as they continued walking towards him.

When the man threw the first punch, he had them for assaulting a police officer. When the second man drew the hunting knife, he was in another fight for his life. He managed to block the punch but was forced to go into a rolling dive to avoid the knife thrust. He tried drawing his .38 but was hit with a solid kick to the ribs. His left arm was still useless, so he rolled with the kick as far under the bushes as he could get. He knew this placed the knife man in an awkward position as he was forced into a crouching position stabbing downward. The assailant came forth as the second man circled to the right. It gave Evan time to draw his revolver and point it at the surprised attackers.

"Okay, on your knees," he ordered. "Down on the ground."

This was it, he realized as he rose to his feet and the hoboes eyed him warily. They would be onto him now, as all Hyatt would have to do was pick up copies of the police reports to see that Carlow's name appeared on both. He had no choice to come out and let Bob Methot take up the trail. Methot wasn't his favorite choice as he was a real cowboy and also had eyes for Roni. However, there was no choice as these two had him made, staring intently to remember every detail of his features.

"Hey, man, we screwed up. We thought you were someone else," one of the big men rumbled.

"Well, I wish I was," Evan scowled. He then got to work his roundhouse knockout kick, first against the jaw of one kneeling man, then the next. He left them sprawled across the grass as he speed-dialed his cell phone to have Bob Methot meet him at Memorial Park as soon as possible.

2330 hours – Veronica and Khalid returned to the warehouse to find Hyatt and the disciples meeting near his office, and they were in a tense and somber mood. Andrew and Philip had black and blue welts on the left side of their faces, but the concern was over the issue that Hyatt had brought before his bodyguards.

"Now is the time for action," Hyatt exhorted them as he paced before where they sat on their cots facing him. "Michaelangelo has completed the work on the paper bombs and we are ready to launch this attack. I tell you, gentlemen, this City will be ground to a halt by noon today as a result of our actions."

"I'll tell you, Ad, I'm not sure if I'm gonna be good with this one," Thomas spoke up, rubbing his beard musingly. "Those Feds are gonna be all over us for something like this, and I can't take another Federal rap. I've got those two priors, and if they nail me with something like this I'm looking at some serious time."

"I'm not good with getting my first one," James spoke out. "I'm good with the money we're making on the streets, and I don't mind doing these little demonstrations to put some weight behind us. Running a risk of being brought into a Federal indictment is where I'll need to draw the line."

"All right, guys, let's dope this one out," Hyatt insisted. "We set the boxes out, it doesn't mean we had anything to do with the manufacture of the counterfeits. Once we walk away, the passers-by are grabbing stuff out of the box, there's no distribution on our part. Plus, all they're gonna have is eleven guys wearing beards and black clothing on tape, if that. If they turn up the heat we just shave the beards and hop a train, just like I said in the beginning. They're gonna take as many bills as possible back to Washington and start investigating how they were forged, that's their standard procedure. They won't give a rat's ass about a bunch of guys who left them out on the curb."

"I say we let our rail dogs do the heavy lifting on this one," Simon insisted. "I'll be more than glad to hire a cab to haul the box out there, but I'm not stepping in front of a camera lens to make the drop." This was met by a round of assenting murmurs from his brethren.

"Okay, then," Hyatt looked up and beckoned Veronika and Khalid to join them. "Eleven Disciples, our Blessed Mother, and the Resolver joined together in this effort. We shall split into teams: five boxes shall be delivered, and two persons shall bring their Followers in a cab along with a box to be dropped at a specified location. I myself will ride along with our new members, and we will make sure that everything goes according to plan."

"Hell, it's almost midnight, how're we gonna round those little shits up before dawn?" John grumbled.

"The boxes will not arrive until 0800," Hyatt assured him. "You'll have plenty of time. I suggest we all get plenty of rest, we have a long day ahead."

Veronika returned to her cot with her mind racing wildly. She had no idea that Hyatt was planning something of this magnitude. She had to figure out a way to notify Evan so he could get some backup on the street to monitor the situation. If they could catch Hyatt or the Disciples red-handed, this counterfeiting scheme would be more than enough to win the gold for her.

The question that was gnawing at her now was how much more she would have to endure to earn the coveted prize. The deprivations, the rape, the risk to her life among these people were taking a psychological and physical toll. They were now crossing the threshold from civil disobedience to a Federal offense, and if they murdered four hoboes over a mere dispute, there was little doubt they might take equally drastic measures to cover these tracks.

She drifted off into a dozing slumber, her tummy churning with trepidation at the thought of what might lie ahead. All she could think of was Evan, and how she would need him more than ever when she set out alongside the Disciples on Hyatt's chaotic mission ahead.

0200 – Evan Carlow had briefed Bob Methot on the situation when he arrived at the IRT Clark Street Station around midnight. Methot was a tall, powerfully-built Irish Cherokee who wore his hair in a Mohawk buzzcut as far as regulation permitted. He was dressed in a grungy black hoodie, jeans and construction boots just as Evan, and jotted down all the information before taking leave of his fellow officer.

"Hey, don't worry, you know me," Methot winked. "I'll be taking real good care of our Roni."

"That's what I'm worried about," Evan frowned.

He reported to Police Plaza shortly afterward, and was met by Lieutenant Shreve and a number of other undercover cops on duty who had been called in as a result of the updated information being supplied by Evan.

"Okay," Shreve switched on a Power Point presentation in a conference room where they had gathered, a display of old mugshots of Adolf Hyatt on an overhead screen. "Here's our rock star. Adolf Vernon Hyatt, born in Cloudcroft, New Mexico, classic sociopath, dropped out of grade school with a 160 IQ. Hit the rails, traveled down to Texas, busted for vagrancy and sent to a number of juvie homes and halfway houses. He escaped dozens of times and finally took off to California where he took a drug bust. They kept him in San Quentin for a while until he got released on parole, then skipped down to New Orleans where they took him down for numerous home improvement scams. He did some time before hitting the Midwest, where he made himself a rep as some kind of transient guru among the next generation of bums and hoboes. He got crowned King of the Hoboes one year at the Annual Hobo Convention in Iowa, and never relinquished the title. Over the years he's built up a power base and it's been reported he's the central figure of a loosely-based gang network. He's brought his act here to the Big Apple, and we think he's taken a turn for the worse."

"My partner Officer Heydrich has come up with a witness to a multiple murder committed about a month ago along the East River," Evan had been brought up to address the group. "There are no other witnesses, no bodies, no weapons, no motive. She's working undercover on the case and has gotten inside Hyatt's circle. I was attacked by a couple of Hyatt's men a few days ago, and those gentlemen are currently in solitary on Rikers Island. Heydrich has witnessed activity indicating the group may be involved in illegal activity in the downtown area of Brooklyn along Flatbush Avenue. While I was tailing Heydrich this evening I was attacked once again, and I disabled the perps before calling in Detective Methot to relieve my position. I'm thinking there's something big going down, and Methot is on standby to activate a surveillance team as soon as he gets a fix on Hyatt's situation."

"That's what you call some deep undercover," one of the detectives joked about Evan's slovenly appearance.

"Okay, cut the crap," Shreve ordered, the Appalachian slope of his large forehead as a ledge over his gold-rimmed glasses. "I want everyone on standby waiting for Methot's call. He'll be reporting directly to me, and if you get an urgent call from my line, drop everything and call in for the detailed message."

0800 - Veronika and Khalid accompanied Hyatt and the Disciples to Water Street beneath the Brooklyn Bridge where they were met at length by a panel truck that pulled onto a parking area not far from the River Café. The Disciples hustled over to the truck and unloaded five cardboard boxes from the rear, waiting for a short while until a fleet of cabs appeared. Five of the cabs were loaded by Disciples and Followers, taking off though one remained behind in awaiting Hyatt, Veronika and Khalid.

Veronika was somewhat concerned that they were being kept under watch by Hyatt himself, yet there would have been little problem for them to escape if physically threatened. She was sure that he would be looking for signs of rebellion from either of them, which would have resulted in him cutting them loose from the inner circle. Obviously they had made a good impression and the Hyatts wanted to keep them, so this would be the test of fire. If they came through this, they would be full-fledged members. Veronica only hoped that this escapade would give him the rope he needed to hang himself.

"Who was that Michaelangelo you were talking about last night?" Veronika wondered. "Was that his truck back there?"

"Michaelangelo is one of the finest artists in the land, though you will never find his name on his work anywhere in America," Hyatt sat back in the spacious yellow cab, large enough for the three of them to sit side-by-side. "He has decorated walls across the nation with paintings so marvelous that they appear in photographed collections at national libraries. When I told him of this project, he was more than happy to come up here to lend a hand. It took him a while, but he has recently printed work guaranteed to make a Treasury agent cry."

Khalid glanced over at Veronika, who arched an eyebrow and gave him a small smile. If only she had a recorder or that wire Evan was talking about.

She had no way of knowing that Bob Methot was on the trail of their cab, following at the prescribed distance in a beat-up 2000 Chevy Vega. He had just managed to stay within range of Veronika and Khalid as they accompanied the Hyatts to the rendezvous with the panel truck. He had copied the license plate number and called it in to Lt. Shreve, and would now stay on Hyatt and Veronika's tail until they arrived at their next destination.

0845 – The taxi arrived in front of a dollar store on Times Square, and the three of them emerged from the cab. Veronika was surprised to see about twenty bums congregated around the street corner to which they had been directed by word of mouth the day before. Hyatt stood atop a box that had been placed there, giving him a commanding view of the bustling sidewalk. A few people stopped and watched as they not only recognized him from the media, but also knew that the homeless community had been demonstrating as of late. They hoped they might somehow become part of an event and even appear on TV.

"Today is yet another Day of Defiance!" Hyatt called out to the growing crowd of spectators. "Today will be yet another day of reckoning for the duplicitous and vacillating Administration that is hoodwinking the people of this City! We have staged demonstrations across the City to no avail. As we speak, there are children out there with no place to sleep, women going without the barest feminine necessities, and men begging in the streets for money for their next meal! We can stand by and tolerate this no longer! If the City will not give you the money to supply your basic needs, then your Resolver will find a way!"

As he spoke, four Followers came out of the crowd and lined themselves up in a protective cordon around Hyatt. He stepped down from the box at length, and the Followers produced box cutters with which they sliced the sealed cartons open. Both Veronika and Khalid marveled at the stacks of dollar bills wrapped neatly inside the box. The Followers began breaking the paper seals on a number of stacks and tossing them haphazardly back into the box as the crowd began gathering closer.

Things started happening quicker than Veronika could keep track of. Bob Methot's Vega double-parked alongside a car about ten yards away from where they stood, and he got out after putting on his emergency lights to pop the hood of the Chevy. Methot had pulled a ski cap down over his brow and Veronika did not recognize him. Hyatt glanced over with a look of concern, but was distracted as his audience was drawn near by the rumors of the money in the box. He kept looking down the street past Methot's car, and at length a brown 1984 Ford Cutlass made a sudden swerve and pulled in front of Methot.

0857 – The men in the Cutlass were staring around frantically, speaking rapidly to each other in a foreign language which could be heard through the open windows of the car. At once a flat-topped patrol car without emergency lights pulled up and hit the strobe lights on the dashboard. Wyatt grabbed Veronika by the hand and led her into the crowd as the Followers made a flying wedge for him towards the subway. Veronika tugged at Khalid's sleeve as he rushed behind them, the two staring back at what was transpiring.

Evan Carlow and two uniformed officers jumped out of the patrol car and dragged the Muslims out of the Cutlass, throwing them against the hood of the car and cuffing their hands behind their back. Methot rushed to join the cops but was grabbed by the front of the shirt by Evan.

"These guys are suicide bombers!" Evan yelled. "This car is rigged!"

"Are you shittin' me?" Methot's eyes widened.

"Quick, the dollar store!" Evan nodded. "Make a hole between these two and I'll smash through!"

"Hey, if it doesn't work, it's been a blast," Methot grinned.

Both he and Methot jumped into their cars as more NYPD patrol cars began blaring their way along Times Square to converge upon the scene. Methot backed into the car behind him to make more room, then turned to ram the car in front of him so as to shove the left bumper into traffic. He then pulled back and surged forth again, shoving the car about a foot from the curb. He then backed up and plowed the exposed right bumper, nearly knocking the car sideways into the traffic lane before backing up again into the car behind him.

He then jumped out of the car and ran into the dollar store, yelling at everyone to leave the store as he held his badge aloft. Evan smirked as he watched Methot bring two Korean women out by the hair before he gunned the engine and floored the gas pedal. The car jumped onto the sidewalk and smashed through the storefront, sending glass and prefabricated materials flying in all directions. He jumped out of the Cutlass as it continued smashing its way through the display shelves and counters, its tires finally getting stalled as they got tangled in debris.

Evan had barely hit the sidewalk when his instincts told him to roll away from the storefront. Just as he did, the Cutlass exploded, sending a shower of merchandise and broken glass back out into the street. Forensics investigators would later determine that there was over a hundred pounds of shrapnel in the back trunk that would have torn into a crowd of bystanders along a fifty-foot perimeter. Carlow and Methot's actions caused the dollar store to be ripped asunder though the lives of dozens of people had been saved.

To their chagrin, Veronika Heydrich was nowhere to be seen. They had lost her trail once again, and this time they had no idea where she would be taken now that an arrest warrant would be out for Adolf Hyatt.

Chapter Ten

It was the Rohypnol again, the date rape bullshit that was all the rage back in the 90s, the cause of so many girls getting knocked up that President Clinton himself made it a Federal offense to slip it into chicks' drinks. The Hyatts were into crap up to their necks by now, and there was no doubt they were going to shave their heads, cut their beards and take the next train out of Dodge. Only there was the last phase of Hyatt's operation that had to be taken care of, one last thing for which the Resolver's ego demanded closure. The three of them met the Disciples back at the warehouse, and she noticed that all the cots were gone. Peter had been pouring wine for everyone as they arrived, and after Veronika and Khalid took a few sips of theirs, they were lost in outer space once more.

"Be sure you keep those two loaded up," Hyatt ordered two of the Disciples as they bound Veronika and Khalid hand and foot. They carried them to the candle-lit ceremonial room where they were dumped in a corner by the door. "The meeting will start at nine, you fellows be sure and bring everyone in."

Veronika laid back on the black-tiled floor, feeling comfortably numb and not overly concerned about what the Hyatts were up to at this particular time. She figured Evan would bring the cavalry charging in sooner or later. She heard the blast from the subway tunnel while the three of them were on the platform, and everyone in the station was hysterical at the thought of being buried alive. Hyatt merely led them onto the oncoming train and they took off to downtown Brooklyn, assuming that whatever happened worked out according to plan.

If she lived through this, she would have this son of a bitch nailed to the wall. Khalid could testify to the assault on a police officer though that might well get kicked out for lack of evidence. She could've come off the field and had her butt checked for DNA samples, but this would work much better. They were going to get him for conspiracy on the counterfeiting charge, and more than likely tie him in with whatever bomb went off after they left the scene. All she had to do was chill out a little bit longer, and everything would work out just fine.

Thoughts of Evan was what was keeping her from passing out. Knowing him, he probably threw himself into the thick of things once he arrived on the scene. Yet everything happened so quick that she doubted he would have figured it all out and moved in before the bomb exploded. She needed to get some news about the blast, which had to be all over the media by now. If she could just wriggle over by the door, she could eavesdrop on them and get all the details. Only she was so stoned that it was all she could do to keep her eyes open.

Veronika reconciled herself to the fact that someone would be on the way very soon. Once Evan blew the whistle on Hyatt, this place would be surrounded by cops, and there would be a nice hot bubble bath waiting for her, and a bottle of champagne in a bucketful of ice right alongside the small table where her shiny gold detective's badge would be sitting.

With all these wonderful thoughts in her head, Veronika soon fell fast asleep.

"We've got this son of a bitch dead to rights," Bob Methot was adamant. "Why don't we go in and take him now?"

"Look, you just came in cold on this thing less than twenty-four hours ago," Evan snapped at they sat in front of Captain Willard's office along with Lieutenant Shreve. "You don't have a feckin' clue as to what's going on here."

"You're probably right, seeing how I got briefed by you."

"All right, guys, there are shit storm warnings in effect, and you can be damned sure it's not gonna start in here," Willard raised his voice. "Now I got Homeland Security scratching at Chief Madden's door, and they're expecting a statement from the White House any time now. Everything's been traced back to Sheik Abdul Hameed, a top executive in Al Qaeda. Right now the official line is that Al Qaeda was taking advantage of the homeless demonstration in Times Square, and that the events are unrelated. The Administration does not want any backlash directed against the homeless community, and the Mayor and the Governor's Office want to be very clear about that. Our surgical procedure is all about cutting Adolf Hyatt out of the social event and nailing him on an unrelated charge. Now, we've got five boxes of one dollar counterfeits totaling one hundred thousand dollars, at twenty grand per box. Only ten percent of these were printed on both sides, and the paper he used is bullshit. In other words, gentlemen, this is not going to Washington. We need to take him down with whatever we can put together without trying to link him to Al Qaeda."

"Okay, I got a rape and four murders you're saying we can't use," Evan grunted. "I also got two assaults on a police officer, plus conspiracy to commit fraud. So you're telling me there's not a drop of glue anywhere to make this stick."

"Dammit, Carlow, you're a five-year man, one of the best on my team," Willard shot back. "You know this guy's gonna have the ACLU on their haunches begging for this case if we brought it to trial with what you got. This guy's got the potential to be the Gandhi of the 21st century. If he beats us in court he becomes a historical figure. If we take him down right, he's just another bum on the street running a scam. So your job is to make sure we can nail him to the wall when we bring him in."

"Another problem I got is that while Bob and I were saving the world at the dollar store, Hyatt went south with Roni and the Indian kid," Evan pointed out.

"We got that covered," Shreve interjected. "We got undercover all over Memorial Park and Brooklyn Heights. Roni and the kid are back at the JW's warehouse, safe and sound. They're just waiting for word from us to take 'em down."

"Okay, I need to touch bases with Roni and see where we stand on getting a grand jury indictment," Evan and Methot rose to leave.

"Our guys on the field are telling us that there's heavy traffic around the warehouse, so apparently the roaches aren't checking out just yet," Shreve assured him. "Bob hasn't been made yet, so maybe he can get up close and find out what's going on before we go barging in."

"Sounds good," the detectives replied as they took their leave. Evan wasn't overjoyed about working with Methot on this, but since they were probably going to get commended together for their work at Times Square, he probably wasn't going to have a better choice. He also knew they were going to have to close it down before Hyatt flew the coop, especially while Roni was still safe and sound. Time was of the essence, and they needed to get this done before it was too late.

Roni was just starting to come to when one of the Disciples came in with a cup and had both her and Khalid take a sip. She was too messed up to consider the fact that it might contain more drugs, and went ahead and swallowed before nodding out again. This time it hit her like a load of bricks, and she was out for a longer period of time. It was not until after dark by the time Peter came into the ceremonial room and pulled them both to a sitting position on the floor.

"Okay, we're getting ready to shut this place down," Peter squatted down alongside then, rubbing his face wearily. "Looks like we've done everything we came here to do. Ad's gonna have a farewell meeting with the Followers, then we're outta here. We just need to make sure you two're not gonna tell any tall tales or give up anything you're supposed to keep secret."

"Hell, you know we're solid," Roni slurred her words with a thick tongue. "We aren't gonna roll over on you. Besides, we don't know shit anyway."

"We ain't gonna give 'em nothin'," Khalid's eyes were glazed. "Nothin'."

"I believe you, my friend," Peter gently helped them to their feet. "C'mon, lemme get you over to the restroom so you can get straightened up. Addy'll be expecting us at the meeting in a bit."

He walked them over to the restroom, and Khalid fell against the wall where he slid and dropped on his butt. Roni went inside and tottered over to a toilet stall, where she went inside, sat down and fell asleep.

A few hours later, the main chamber was filled with Followers and Believers as the Disciples began debriefing their gang members. There was over fifty men in attendance, and each of them was distracted by the repercussions of the incident of that day. Police were swarming the Brooklyn Heights area, and suspicious characters were getting rousted left and right. The Disciples were seeing lots of strange faces in the crowds, and with their Special Forces training, they were growing more and more concerned. Finally Hyatt was sure that everyone had mustered up in calling the meeting to order at last.

"Brethren, at long last we bring this enterprise to its conclusion," Hyatt had the curtains drawn back in the ceremonial room, the great pentagram shining behind him for theatrical effect. "What we have accomplished here will remain a part of urban legend here in Brooklyn, and we will leave footprints behind us for our brethren to follow. We have shown this corrupt Administration and the evil Government what happens when people unite in a common cause. We have also demonstrated what the oppressed people of the world can accomplish when we work together against the exploitive corporations of America!"

"I hope you're not sayin' we had anything to do with that shit at Times Square, Ad," Peter spoke for the rest of them as they crowded around the doorframe where Hyatt stood.

"Any blow we strike against the proletariat is a good hit, my brothers!" Hyatt assured them. "However, don't let those cops outside make you believe we are terrorists or insurgents in any way, shape or form! Governments have been dragging down the people since the beginning of time, calling citizens enemies of the State if they speak against injustice! No, we are martyrs, and the true enemies are those among us who would betray us to the exploiters and the predators!"

At once the large gathering watched in wonderment as the two figures were brought before Hyatt. Veronika and Khalid were clad only in their robes, having been thrown into the shower to sober up. They were both dazed and confused, and were filled with trepidation as Hyatt stood between them with his hands on their shoulders.

"Now, the bloodhounds that chase the wolves never stop and think how closely one canine is related to another," Hyatt smiled at his followers. "The hunters forget that the dogs of war are one of a kind, and regardless whether you pit one against the other, brother will not turn against brother. Our veteran brothers reached out to veterans they served alongside, and soon we found out that Veronika Heydrich is working with the NYPD!"

Bob Methot had managed to sneak into the warehouse along with the dealers and go-fers that had been recruited by the Followers, and he had his phone set to text as he remained along the perimeter of the gathering. When Veronika had been revealed, he hit a key on his phone which immediately alerted Evan stationed outside.

"Now, I will not harm a cop and turn the wrath of the NYPD against all who stand together in this place," Hyatt produced a .38 Smith and Wesson from his waistband while still holding Khalid's shoulder. "However, I will show this cop just how we deal with liars and traitors, and if any of you wish to deal further with this lady pig, this Jezebel, well…here she is. And think careful, my friends, lest she remembers your face and goes back to report that you were part of this!"

With that, Adolf pulled his .38, jammed it against Khalid's head and pulled the trigger. Veronika screamed as the blood spurted from the other side of Khalid's head before he toppled to the floor.

The entire group was thrown into pandemonium as the gunshot was deafening in the small room. The Disciples were obviously not prepared for this as they began looking for exit routes. Methot dropped to one knee and drew his weapon just as the front door crashed open.

"It's over, Hyatt!" Evan rushed into room and dropped into a triangle stance, his Glock pointed at Hyatt's head. "You're under arrest, put your hands in the air! You have the right to remain silent, and anything you say can and will be held against you!"

"Do you know where you are, you son of a bitch?" Hyatt laughed derisively. "You're in my world, this is my kingdom! In your world, you give to Caesar what is Caesar's! In my world, your ass belongs to me!"

"Hands above your head, Hyatt!" Evan screamed. "Don't make me do this!"

"All right, fellows," Hyatt instructed the hoboes standing between him and Evan, "just come in on him slowly, slowly. Don't make him do anything he doesn't want to do."

"Hyatt," Evan yelled, "Veronika Heydrich is an undercover police officer! She has compiled evidence and will give testimony to this murder as well as all the other crimes, State and Federal, you have committed! Put your hands on your fuggin' head!"

"I got your back, Evan," Methot called from the other side of the crowd, pointing his pistol at Hyatt, causing many of the Followers to duck for cover. "Drop the gun, Hyatt!"

"I am walking out of here and I am disappearing, gentlemen!" Hyatt grabbed her by the back of the neck, holding her as a shield with the revolver pointed at her head. "Put your guns down or I'll put one right in her head! I just killed that kid, I'm all it, it won't make any difference if she goes too!"

"All right, you son of a bitch!" Methot set his gun on the concrete floor as the crowd parted before him. "Just let her go and you can walk right out. Just let her go!"

"She's walking me to the door, boys!" Hyatt chortled. "She's my ticket to freedom, and you'd better do as I say if you don't want to see my ticket get punched!"

"Last warning, Hyatt," Evan stepped closer as the group continued to fall back before the undercover cops. "Drop the gun and put your hands behind your head!"

"I'm walking out, boys, and you'll never hear from me again!" Hyatt cried triumphantly. "The King of the Hoboes is moving on, and he leaves his name to carry on!"

Evan Carlow took his shot. He aimed and fired a bullet at over thirty feet, just over Veronika's shoulder, grazing her neck and burning through her hair as it hit Hyatt square in the face, just below his left eye. The King of the Hoboes dropped his gun from his lifeless fingers, loosing his grip on Veronika's shoulder as he fell through the doorway to the floor

behind him. Veronika stared in shock as Hyatt's right arm sprawled above his head, seeming to point at the pentagram that flickered in the candlelight of the shadowy chamber.

Bob Methot's first instinct was to play the hero and run to Veronika's side, but he would not ignore Evan's safety in doing so. He remained in firing position as he watched the vagrants charging for the door. Despite what Hyatt thought, deep down these people were all homeless people just trying to make it on the street. He was just another three-card monte dealer turning his box over and tossing the cards away when the cops drove up. The show was over, and these guys would be back outside looking for a decent place to sleep tonight.

"Roni!" Evan was the first to reach her, nimbly stepping around Khalid as he took her in his arms.

"Oh my gosh, be careful, you're gonna hurt Khalid!" her voice quavered through the narcotic haze, still under the influence of Hyatt's sedatives.

"Let's just get you out of here," Evan put his arm around her shoulder, seeing she was naked under the robe, blood pouring from the superficial wound on her neck. "Bob, get an ambulance in here!"

"On the double," he assured them as sirens began whooping outside, the strobe lights of police cars on the scene flashing through the opened doors.

"Evan, stop, don't leave Khalid," she pleaded.

"He's gone, baby," Evan walked her past him, a large pool of blood around Khalid as his eyes stared lifelessly at the ceiling. Yet Evan could not help but stare at the huge organ hanging limply between his legs. Out of respect, he bent down and flicked the boy's robe over to cover his privates.

Outside the warehouse, most of the Disciples had fled into the darkness as the Followers sacrificed themselves, walking straight into the police ranks surrounding the building to be arrested. The Disciples would look back with satisfaction at how their hand-picked troops remained loyal to the end. The Internet and the media would speculate for months as to whether Adolf Hyatt had any connection to the Times Square bomb plot, or if he had just been forced into a desperate situation by an Administration and a New York Police Department bent on destroying what they could not control.

Though his legend lived on, the remains of Adolf Hyatt went unclaimed and were tossed into a common grave along the Meadowlands in New Jersey.

Veronika Heydrich was treated for her wounds at Long Island College Hospital on Hicks Street in Brooklyn while Evan Carlow and Bob Methot were summoned to Police Plaza for debriefing by Chief Madden and Captain Willard. New York City was still on red alert over the failed bombing on Times Square, and the killings of Khalid Sangani and Adolf Hyatt were barely making the second page of local newspapers. The papers were calling it a dispute between homeless activists, and the police were content to place it on the back burner as a pending investigation while the details of the Times Square bombing were being sorted out.

Chief Madden himself visited Veronika at her hospital room Brooklyn along with Captain Willard. He gave her the coveted detective's badge along with three weeks' medical leave, and would put her in for a service medal once the Hyatt investigation was concluded.

"You've always been one of my best undercover officers, and I know you're gonna be one of my best detectives," Madden smiled as he reached over and patted her hand. The high-ranking officers sat alongside her bed and had brought a dozen pink roses for her bedside.

"I'm gonna make you proud," she smiled back. She had a huge gauze pad taped to her neck, the wound treated as a second-degree burn.

"I'm sure you will," they rose to leave. Willard would have blushed with embarrassment had it not been for his ebon skin as Madden leaned over and kissed Veronika's cheek.

Veronika took a cab back to her Prince Street loft, arriving about 9 AM. Her mind was racing a mile a minute as she tried to assimilate all that had happened over the past forty-eight hours. She placed her gold badge on top of the dining table in her kitchenette and went over to her cappuccino machine on the kitchen counter, setting up a fresh pot in trying to get her head together.

She could not believe that Khalid was dead. The thought of his tragic life having ended with no chance for redemption was heartbreaking. She considered the thought of him being here with her, rehashing all they had gone through together in less than a week. Even though he screwed her while she was passed out, she would have forgiven him for that. He could have run off at any time, especially after getting raped by the Hyatts. He could have given up after meeting Evan and finding out she was a cop. He might have even managed to sneak out after they were drugged after the Times Square bombing. Even before then, he could have run off in the crowded subway train on the way back to Brooklyn. Hyatt could not have possibly stopped him. Yet he would not leave Veronika. He stayed with her to the very end.

She still did not know all the details of the terrorist bombing, and wondered if Hyatt had anything to do with it. They had taken their funny money to five different locations around the City, and doubtlessly the actions created mob scenes and chaos in each vicinity. Still, she would not turn on the TV just yet. She needed to be alone with her thoughts, despite the fact that she was finally back home after a week of utter deprivation. Hyatt had sacrificed himself for his cause, and she was wondering if she had done likewise.

She wanted to reevaluate her own core values and her own principles. She needed to rethink how and why she had placed such a value on that gold badge. It sat proudly on the table, yet it was almost as a reproach to her driving ambition, a rebuke and a disgrace to her self-worth. She had endured utter degradation to earn the badge, and could have pulled out to have waited for a more opportune time and place. Yet her impatience and pride compelled her to go through hell and high water for this. She had the badge, but Khalid was dead, and she could not ever forget the shame or disgrace of the gang rape. No one would ever stand trial for it, no one would ever face retribution. The Disciples had become ghosts that disappeared from the earth along with Adolf Hyatt.

She heard the key in the lock, and was sitting at the table with a cup of cappuccino when Evan walked in. He looked as if he had gone for days without sleep, and his right arm was still crooked like a crab's claw. He looked impassively at the badge sitting on the table before her, as if it was some kind of totem that was now redefining who she was. He walked over to the window and stared down at the bustling street below.

"Gee, that's a real warm welcome back. Aren't you gonna congratulate me?"

"We've gone through hell for that damn thing," he continued looking out the window. The Disciples had dropped one of the boxes off along the Avenue of the Americas, about six blocks away from Veronika's loft. It started a near-riot as the crowd tore the box open and the counterfeit bills were scattered all over the street. Two people ran into oncoming traffic, and one of them was killed instantly. Stores throughout the area closed down in order to remain uninvolved with the chaos as people were running into stores trying to make purchases as soon as possible with the phony bills. The police finally cordoned off the area and sent squads of officers in to collect the remaining notes that had been trampled on the streets and sidewalks. "I would've gone ahead and given you mine if it were possible."

"Too bad it doesn't work that way. Women always have to go the hard way to get where they want to be. It's always been like that."

"There should've been a point when we drew the line," he leaned up against the wall by the window, his voice husky. "The whole deal was bullshit. We had no way to communicate, no chance to compare notes. I wouldn't have even found out what happened to you if you hadn't come back here with Khalid."

"Hey, shit happens, and we made it, we got through it. It wasn't like I was a virgin, or I suffered some kind of trauma. It could've been worse, they could've forced me against my will with no drugs. Now that would have been seriously screwed up."

"Well, I'm glad it hurt me a lot more than it hurt you," he managed.

"No it doesn't. I'm just dealing with it better than you are."

"Yeah, the whole situation, apparently," he rubbed his head exasperatedly. "I lost that kid. That bothers me a whole lot more."

"You didn't lose him. Hyatt murdered him."

"He wouldn't have stayed in if it wasn't for me," Veronika wiped a tear from her eye.

"If I'm not mistaken, he raped you too, didn't he?"

"It wasn't the same, it was like leaving a pound of steak on the table with a dog in the house," her voice broke. "I'm not excusing what he did, but I can understand it. If you had such a problem with it, why didn't you bust him? At least he'd still be alive."

"Because it was all about you," he vented. "It's always got to be your way, no matter how it ends up, right or wrong. If we have a train wreck, as long as you can find a way to salvage something, then all's well that ends well in your book. Whenever I try to give you some advice or stop you from ending up in a mess somewhere, it's always like I'm against you, like I'm holding you back. Now you've got your badge, but at what cost?"

"Why'd you take that shot, Evan?" tears streamed down her cheeks. It was as if all the tension was finally releasing itself after a week in hell. "You could've killed me."

"I wanted it to be over," he admitted. "I didn't want Hyatt pulling that robe off you and walking you down the street to make us jump through hoops for him. Think about it, why did he drug you two and strip you naked? He was probably anticipating a hostage situation, or worse. He already killed Khalid, how could've we put it past the sick bastard to have pulled you into that room and shot you on top of that pentagram?"

"Bob Methot was in the room, he might've had a better shot."

"And you think he could've done better?"

"Don't start that jealous crap. I'm just saying, if you had been off an inch to the left I'd be dead right now."

"Well, I don't miss. I had better plans."

"Like what?"

He wordlessly pulled a small velvet box out of the pocket of his hoodie and put it on the table in front of Veronika, then headed for the door.

"So that's it? No bended knee or anything?" she sniffled, wiping her eyes.

"Woman, I've been on my knees for the last two years," he said as he walked out. "It's time I stretched my legs a bit."

As he closed the door behind him, she stared contemplatively at the box next to the badge on the table before her. Just last week, it was as if these were the most important things she could want in life. Now they were here in her possession, and she could not help but wonder how much she lost in getting them. She started wondering if she had ever really considered the cost, and whether she had ever questioned what kind of person would have taken such risks. She began to wonder if she knew who she really was.

She had always seen her fabrications as a slight flaw, like other women had moles or birthmarks on their faces. Only now it had finally caught up to her, and she wondered whether she had started lying to herself. She wondered whether she had created a Veronika that was no longer the person she was trying to be, the person Chief Madden kept a favored eye on, the one that Evan Carlow had fallen in love with. She now had to ask herself whether the woman she had reconstructed had the same qualities that made others love her. She wondered whether she was distancing herself from that person to create a superwoman that could not be loved, who refused to be loved.

She considered the fact that possibly God allowed her to be put out on the street in some sort of ritual of self-realization. She didn't consider herself a religious person, but had enough of a Catholic upbringing to assign blame or credit for things happening in life to God rather than fate. It made her feel more reassured in thinking that things in her life happened for a reason, rather than as an outcome in some cosmic crap shoot. If God had sent her out for a reason, then she could not possibly have endured what she had without asking why.

Perhaps it was all about seeing how strong of a person she was. If someone would have suggested that she go out on the street and endure the indignities she had suffered, she would have laughed in their face. Yet when all this gold was set before her, she had found it easier to set her standards aside to stake her claims. Now that she had won all her prizes, the question was how it had changed her. Had it proved or strengthened her character, or weakened it by merely satisfying her lusts and desires, making it so she would still want more?

She went into the bathroom and drew a hot bubble bath, then headed to the kitchen and poured herself a glass of Asti Spumanti. She sat and soaked for nearly an hour until the water grew tepid, then got out and toweled herself, wondering what she would do with three weeks' time off. Maybe they would give Evan some time off too, maybe not. She was not going to call him until he called to apologize. She lost a lot along the way here, but she still had her pride. Maybe too much of it, she realized. Maybe she needed to lose a little bit more to be the kind of person she needed to be.

She absently went to the bathroom and got out a pair of scissors. She sat naked on the stool in front of the bathroom mirror and began trimming her golden locks, first a little along the sides, then thicker strands to try and keep it even. She considered the fact that when people didn't know what they were doing, they had to cut off more and more to straighten out the mess they made. Maybe that was the allegory here.

By the time she was finished, most of her golden fleece was piled on the floor, and the woman in the mirror looked as if she had escaped from a concentration camp. She decided she would leave it right where it was, and if Evan came back and saw this he would have a fit and fall back in it. Maybe she was punishing him as much as she was punishing herself.

She went into the bedroom and picked out a black T-shirt, jeans and sneakers, along with a small travel bag and the bare essentials she never picked up while she was with the Hyatts. She stuck the cheap plastic comb in her pocket along with her wallet. This time she would have a few bucks in her pocket, some ID and some plastic in case she got into a real jam. Most likely she wouldn't. It was a lot easier to come out when you had a choice of staying in or not.

She put on the cheap black hoodie along with her New Jersey Devils cap, and locked the apartment up, slipping her keys in her pocket as she headed for the elevator. She thought of the descent to the grade floor as symbolic in itself. She would learn a lot more about herself before she took the ride back up to her private nirvana again.

And so she set out to solve the puzzle that Veronika Heydrich had become.

Other books by John Reinhard Dizon

- Nightcrawler-series

  - Nightcrawler
  - Tryzub - Nightcrawler II
  - The Plague - Nightcrawler III

- Generations

- Strange Tales

- Tiara

- Vampir

Lightning Source UK Ltd.
Milton Keynes UK
UKHW041058161120
373486UK00016B/169